The Football Boy Wonder Chronicles 1-3

Martin Smith

In loving memory of David Smith.

Charlie Fry and the
Penalty Shootout

1. HOT AND BOTHERED

It was boiling – the hottest summer anyone could remember. It had been so warm the small patch of grass outside Crickledon Sports Centre had turned yellow.

In the sunshine, a long queue of kids waited noisily outside the sports centre.

The line was long. It snaked along the wall of the old building and around the corner.

Charlie Fry stood in the middle of the queue with pals Peter Bell and Joe Foster.

Peter and Charlie were often mistaken for brothers. They were both small and skinny with short blonde hair.

Joe, on the other hand, loomed over them with muscular shoulders and brown hair that made him stand out from the other two.

The best friends talked quietly and ignored the obvious stares.

By now the Football Boy Wonder was used to being the centre of attention.

Everybody knew about The Boy Who Never Missed – and his footballing exploits for Hall Park Magpies last season.

That freak lightning bolt a year ago had a lot to answer for.

Only a handful of people knew Charlie's big secret: the lightning bolt had somehow imprinted the target from a flick football app into his mind.

Now – with the help of the target inside his mind – the ball would go wherever he decided. It only took the blink of an eye.

The gift had changed Charlie Fry's life. The small blonde-haired whizz-kid had become a marked man but it did not bother him.

He was playing football with his friends – and loving it.

That was all that mattered.

They knew a fair few of the other players too.

Wrecka, who was Peter and Charlie's captain at Hall Park Magpies, was one of the first to come over to say hello. He had turned up to play with a group of his school mates.

This was a competition no-one wanted to miss. The Crickledon Under 14s Five-a-Side tournament took place twice a year.

And it was a big deal.

Charlie, Peter and Joe had been playing in the tournament for two years but had never got past the group stages.

The competition was tough – particularly with older kids playing too. But the gang was confident this year would be different.

"Where are they?" Charlie checked his watch for the umpteenth time.

"Relax, Fry-inho. They'll be here," replied Pete as he leaned against the warm bricks of the sports centre.

Joe looked at his phone.

"I dunno, Pete. Annie is hardly ever late, is she? Anyway, how are you feeling Boy Wonder?"

Charlie hid a little smile.

Joe always asked about his friend's cystic fibrosis, no matter what the situation.

"I'm not too bad, thanks. Have done physio early and feel fine."

Charlie's illness meant he had to clear his lungs of horrible gunge every morning and night.

Exercise was great – so football was the perfect way of helping him, as long as he didn't overdo it.

It was 1.40pm.

The doors opened at 1.45pm and teams had to register before the 2pm deadline, when the first match would kick off.

Teams had to have a minimum of four players.

They were waiting for Annie Cooper, Emma Tysoe, Billy Savage and Darren 'Mudder' Bunnell.

Joe had signed for United after his heroics for Hall Park Rovers last season so he wasn't allowed to play in case he got injured.

Today he was planning to be the team's manager, although his squad only consisted of Peter and Charlie at the moment.

Out of nowhere, something flashed between Peter and Charlie.

A group of larger boys and girls – probably 14 and dressed in green shirts and socks – roared with laughter.

The tallest stood in front of them and pointed.

"I won't miss next time, Boy Wonder."

Charlie didn't answer.

And for once, neither did Peter or Joe.

Simon Crown was far bigger than they were – even Joe.

His team – The Page Boys – had ruled the indoor five-a-side competition for years.

With brown spiky hair and long gangly legs, the big teenager – known as Crowny – was mean and tough.

And he loved to wind up the opposition, particularly people he deemed to be competition.

A door opened behind Simon. It was one of the organisers.

"Registration is now open. Entry is £2 per person.

"Teams must be registered before 2pm … and no-one older than 14 is allowed to play. Is that all clear?"

The crowd murmured in agreement.

Charlie noticed the man looked directly at Crowny and his cronies as he spoke.

From their smug looks, Charlie knew they were still young enough to enter.

His heart sank a little.

Even with the magic target floating around his mind, he was unsure if they could stop the power of Crowny's all-conquering team.

Kids began to file through the building's rickety old silver turnstile.

Charlie, Peter and Joe allowed people behind them in the queue to go past.

Within minutes, they were last in line.

Charlie checked his watch: 1.50pm.

As the last few players waited to go inside, a car turned into the car park.

Seconds later, Annie jumped out as she hastily tied her hair into a ponytail.

She was alone.

Charlie scratched his head in confusion.

"Annie? Where is everyone?"

Annie slammed the car door shut and waved farewell to the woman driving the car.

She turned back to the boys as the car began to pull away and pushed a stray strand of long brown hair out of her eyes.

"I'm really sorry.

"No-one else is coming."

2. QUICK DECISIONS

"WHAT?"

Peter's face had turned bright red. He looked as if he was about to burst.

Joe, as ever, kept a cool head: "What's happened, Annie?"

Annie shook her head and her words tumbled out in a rush: "I'm not too sure. Emma is ill. She has a sickness bug and hasn't slept, so obviously she can't play.

"Billy isn't answering his phone. I've rung him, text and even been to his house. No answer. That idiot is the reason I'm late."

Joe nodded. "Okay. What about Mudder though?"

Annie sighed and rolled her eyes: "Oh, he is the biggest bonehead of the lot."

The boys looked confused but did not reply.

Annie continued: "He is going on holiday today. He thought he was going next week and had not realised his mistake until his mum asked if he was packed. He got his Wednesdays mixed up. He left for the airport about an hour ago."

There was a moment of silence.

And then Charlie sniggered: "What a pilchard."

Peter and Joe looked at him and both began laughing too. Only Mudder could forget he was going on holiday.

Joe checked his phone again. Time was against them. It was 1.52pm.

Where would they find new players at such short notice?

They were now the only people outside the sports centre – everyone else was inside and preparing for the tournament to begin.

Peter picked up his bag.

"Well, it was a nice idea while it lasted. I'm going home. I hate getting beaten by Crowny and his bunch of morons anyway."

Charlie grabbed the bag from Peter and plonked it back on the concrete pathway. "No wait. I've got an idea."

The others looked at him.

"It might work or it might not but we have to give it a go. Go inside and get us registered – I'll stand out here so they can see we have four players but I need to make a quick call."

Peter scratched his head. "Four players? We only have three

though."

Joe understood what Charlie was thinking. He spoke up before Charlie could reply.

"He means we need to pretend that I'm playing. We can always add another couple of players if Charlie's plan comes off."

Charlie nodded and moved away to make the phone call.

Joe and Peter picked up their bags and walked with Annie through the old turnstile into the building.

As usual, it stunk of sweat and cheap deodorant.

Two men wearing bright red Crickledon Sports Centre T-shirts sat behind the registration desk.

They checked their watches as the gang approached.

The older man spoke: "Leaving it a bit close, eh fellas?"

Then he spotted Annie and mumbled: "… oh, and lady."

"I'm sorry but you will need another player. We only take teams of four players or more."

Joe nodded: "Yes, our fourth player is outside on his phone. Here's the cash for me and him."

He flicked out a hand lazily in Charlie's direction before sliding the coins on to the table.

The man looked at the shape of Charlie through the frosted glass window.

"Is that…."

Peter interrupted. "Charlie Fry? Yes, it's the one and only."

The two men looked at each other with raised eyebrows.

"Well, well, well. Today should be interesting indeed. It is £2 entry fee each please. What is your team name?"

Annie piped up: "You Know The Score."

They always had the same name. The man scribbled down the information. "Okay, you have been placed in League Two."

Charlie wandered into the foyer and let out a small sigh of relief.

Wrecka's team had been placed in League One – so thankfully they would avoid them.

However his relief soon turned to dread.

The official continued: "Your league has four teams in it and the top two qualify. You will be playing your first match at 2.10pm against … The Page Boys."

Peter groaned.

They were about to face Crowny's lot with only three players.

3. FAMILIAR FACES

"Who paid my entry fee?"

Joe replied: "I did."

Charlie dug into his pocket and passed the pound coins over to his friend. "Thank you."

The team moved past the ground-floor changing room doorway and followed the staircase up to the first floor.

They knew the route well. They had spent plenty of time here.

During the five-a-side tournaments, the players waited in a huge room that was popular with parties and charity events.

One side had a large viewing gallery overlooking the pitch, while a row of windows allowed people to look down on the centre's squash courts.

All the corners had long been taken by opposition teams so Charlie and his friends sat down in the centre of the room.

Peter nudged Charlie in the ribs.

"So? How did your mystery call work out?"

Charlie shrugged: "They're on their way."

A strange voice stopped Peter from finding out more.

"Hello. What are you guys doing here?"

Gary Bradshaw had played alongside Charlie, Peter and Annie at Hall Park Magpies.

He was a tidy player but always seemed to lack confidence.

The stocky defender dreaded matches because he always feared he would make a mistake or score an own goal.

Peter jumped to his feet and strangled Bradders with a bear hug.

"We are trying to work out how not to get thrashed down there," Peter said as he nodded in the direction of the pitch after letting Bradders go.

"Don't suppose you fancy playing for us?"

Bradders scratched his head. "Well, I guess I could. My dad works here so I normally just come and hang around. I've never played in a five-a-side tournament though."

He flicked his head behind him. Charlie peered over Bradders' shoulder. The main tournament organiser had a long grey beard and was intently watching the first game kick off – he had no idea that he was Gary's dad.

Annie got to her feet. "Come on, Gary. We need you."

A loud cheer erupted from the gallery area followed by kids pounding the thick glass. One of the teams had scored.

Gary looked around for his dad again.

When he turned back to Charlie, he smiled.

"Let's do it. I'll just go and tell my dad.

"I always bring my trainers and shin pads just in case, so I'll grab them. What colour do you wear?"

Joe had been waiting for this question.

"We wear blue, of course! Do you think Charlie would let us wear anything else? I mean wearing green for Magpies must kill him! He's not going to wear any other colour, given a choice."

As he spoke, Joe rummaged in his bag and pulled out a spare training top.

He flung the blue shirt at Bradders.

"You've got two minutes. We'll meet you downstairs."

Bradders caught the top and smiled.

In a flash, he was off and heading towards his father.

Charlie unzipped his tracksuit jacket to reveal his blue shirt underneath.

Peter and Annie had also turned up prepared. There was need for a trip to the changing room. They were ready to face Crowny's mob – except there were still only four of them.

The sports centre's old speaker system crackled into life.

"Would The Page Boys and You Know The Score make their way to the hall's doors for the next match?"

Charlie smiled at the others.

Peter scowled. "Fry, where's this surprise?"

Charlie shrugged. "No idea. Hopefully he'll be downstairs when we get down there."

Within seconds, they were down the stairs. Joe followed a few paces behind. Gary waited by the doors as he attempted to make Joe's large shirt fit.

It was not going too well – he was far too short. And standing next to him was their new recruit: Charlie's little brother Harry.

The boy – who looked just like his older brother – could not keep the huge smile off his face.

Peter stopped on the last step.

"You have got to be kidding."

4. BIG CHOICES

"Charlie!"

Harry spotted his brother and dashed towards him at top speed.

"Hey buddy," Charlie replied, looking a touch embarrassed as Harry tried to hug him in front of everybody.

"I'm going to score loads of goals. I told you I was easily good enough!"

Harry was beaming with excitement.

"Look after him Charlie."

Charlie's dad stood nearby. Liam Fry gave his older son a pat on the back and headed up the stairs to watch the game.

"Sure will, dad."

Charlie frog-marched his brother to stand next to Bradders and then stood a couple of metres away from them, deep in thought.

Peter, Joe and Annie joined him immediately.

They spoke at the same time – no-one listened to the other.

"He's too young, Charlie!"

"Harry can't face Crowny and his mob. They'll destroy him – and us."

"This is not one of your better ideas, Fry-inho."

They were serious.

All three of them looked truly worried by his brainwave to allow Harry to replace Mudder.

Charlie took a deep breath. Harry was nearly eight. At 12, the rest of the team were much older.

Charlie knew Harry was a good player.

They had played enough football in the back garden over the years. And yes, he could hold his own against Charlie but his big brother was small too.

The Football Boy Wonder may have been the player everyone was watching but it had nothing to do with his height.

Charlie was easily one of the smallest players in the competition – and Harry barely came up to his shoulder.

Yet Harry always wanted to play football with Charlie and his friends. This was his big chance.

But Charlie could understand why the others were concerned.

Crowny and the rest of The Page Boys would not go easy on him.

If anything, they would target Harry.

It was Bradders who broke the silence.

"Right, I'm set. Who is playing where?"

A whistle blew. The first game had finished.

The teams burst out of the hall – a rush of conversation and steaming bodies as they trooped towards the stairs for a well-earned drink.

It was nearly game time.

Charlie did not answer Bradders' question.

He looked at Peter and Annie instead.

Peter puffed out his cheeks and ran a hand through his hair.

"I'll go in goal and Annie can take her usual place in defence."

He pointed at Gary: "Bradders, you can help Charlie out in midfield and … Harry, you go up front."

Bradders pulled a face.

"Err, what about Joe?"

Joe shook his head.

"Nah, I can't. Now I'm with United, they say I can't play without their permission. So I'll be the manager today.

"And as the manager, my first decision is … to swap Peter and Bradders. Peter, we need you on the pitch – and you're a rubbish goalkeeper."

Joe's lame joke made everyone smile, even Peter.

"Everyone happy with that?"

Bradders nodded happily and leaned over to take the goalkeeper gloves from Joe.

Harry could barely hide his excitement.

Peter and Annie nodded but said nothing more.

"Come on, let's do this."

Peter went first, pulling open the door to allow the rest of the team through.

As he did so, a wall of noise erupted behind them.

Charlie grabbed Harry.

They both got flattened against the cold brick wall as The Page Boys leapt down the stairs and charged through the open door at full pelt.

Both Joe and Annie were knocked flying.

Peter was trapped behind the door until Crowny's team were inside the hall.

The Page Boys had arrived.

5. AWAY DAY

Crickledon Sports Centre's main hall was like almost every other in the country. It hosted sports throughout the week: five-a-side, basketball, dodgeball, judo, karate. There were also markings for badminton courts on the floor, worn away from years of use.

There were battered five-a-side goals at each end of the hall.

The indoor goals were far smaller than normal goal frames – the crossbar only came up to Charlie's chin.

Five-a-side was completely different to the outdoor version.

The Page Boys had gathered around the small goal nearest to the door so Charlie sprinted towards the far end of the pitch.

Alongside him, Harry waved to their dad watching high above.

Peter called their team together into a small huddle.

"Right, we know we are going to find this tough. They are going to come out fast and try to steamroller us. Tackle as hard as you can and stay on your feet. The match only lasts four minutes so the longer we can keep the scores level the better.

"And remember, we haven't got any subs – so no-one get too exhausted that they can't continue."

He looked directly at Charlie as he spoke. Out of instinct, Charlie coughed and swallowed the ball of gunge that arrived into his mouth.

He cleared his throat: "I told Joe and you earlier: I am fine."

The Boy Wonder was telling the truth.

He would never be 'well' like the others – but today he did not feel ill – and that was as good as it got for him.

Peter held up his hands. "Fair enough, Charlie. Let's do this. And Harry … try to do the best you can."

Harry nodded but did not say anything. Charlie could tell his little brother's excitement had faded and had been replaced by nerves.

Bradders jogged over towards the goal while Peter, Harry and Annie lined up in their positions.

Charlie walked towards the centre of the pitch for kick-off.

Two corners of the hall were sealed off by wooden benches.

These were areas laid out for the subs to sit in.

Joe sat alone behind the bench nearest to Bradders' goal. He gave Charlie a thumbs-up when he saw the Boy Wonder look over.

The other bench was a completely different story.

The Page Boys must have had at least three subs waiting to come on and a whole gaggle of girls supporting them too.

And they were all wearing green shirts to match their team's colours and were so noisy: shouting; laughing; whistling.

Charlie felt like it was an away match.

The ref – a member of the sports centre staff – held a whistle and the match ball – a fluffy green ball, which had been specifically made to be used indoors. Crowny towered over Charlie.

The ref spoke quickly: "Right, the rules are simple. No kicking the ball over head height. No headers. And no-one is allowed inside the semi-circle around each goal – apart from the goalkeepers, who are not allowed outside the area either.

"The match lasts four minutes: two minutes each way. You can make three subs but I need to be told when you want change. All clear?"

Charlie nodded. Crowny just grinned and said nothing.

The ref continued: "Great. Let's get this show on the road."

He blew the whistle and dropped the ball.

BANG!

Crowny's shoulder crashed into Charlie and knocked him over. Seconds later Harry joined him on the floor. Charlie looked to the ref. He was watching the play, not looking at the pile of bodies on the floor.

Peter and Annie raced towards the bulky teenager together – but it was not enough.

Crowny crashed a shot straight towards the bottom corner. It zipped through Peter's legs and flew into the net before Bradders had even seen it.

1–0.

The Page Boys' bench exploded with joy. Crowny stood alone in the corner near Joe with both arms in the air.

The ref blew as Charlie picked himself and Harry up.

His little brother dusted himself down without complaint.

So much for keeping things nice and tight, Charlie thought as he got ready for the ball to be dropped again.

Crowny winked at Charlie as he took up his position again.

"Not so special."

6. CRYING GAME

The words were whispered but Charlie heard them clearly enough.

He gritted his teeth and prepared for more rough treatment … but it did not happen.

Charlie's leg shot out the moment the ball left the ref's hand.

The ball flew into The Page Boys' half but, as Charlie began to move after it, Crowny blocked him and sent him back to the floor.

"Foul!"

Charlie shouted to the ref, who simply told him to get up.

As he did so, Ryan Cage, one of The Page Boys' best players, slipped past Harry's attempt at a tackle and burst forward.

Suddenly green shirts were flooding forward from all areas leaving Peter and Annie completely outnumbered.

They didn't waste it. Cage drew Annie towards him before firing the ball against the wall.

The rebound flew across the pitch and into the area.

It was too fast for Bradders, who desperately dived forward to intercept the cross but could not gather it cleanly.

And there was an unmarked Crowny waiting on the other side of the semi-circle to tap the spilled ball into the empty net.

2–0.

This time the celebration was even louder.

"Easy! Easy! Easy!"

Everyone on The Page Boys' bench was dancing and singing as the teams lined up again.

Peter replaced Charlie for the kick-off this time. The switch made no difference.

With a flick of his long legs, Crowny won the ball with ease and passed back to his team – who played keep-ball as Harry and Charlie attempted to close them down.

Finally, the ref blew for half-time. Two minutes completed and two more still to go. Charlie's team did not utter a word as the teams switched round.

The Page Boy supporters were now right next to Bradders' goal – and made a racket with plenty of whoops and shrieks.

All their subs were ready to come on – fresh legs for the second half with the game already virtually sewn up.

After all, You Know The Score had barely touched the ball during the first half, let alone manage to threaten The Page Boys' goal.

The ref blew again and the new players raced on to the pitch.

The departing players exchanged high-fives and pats on the back from the gaggle of girls standing behind the bench.

Annie took a turn at kick-off – but, yet again, it was Crowny who came away with the ball.

A fancy turn took the older boy away from Annie, who was now hopelessly out of position, and allowed him the time to look for a target.

One of the new players was haring down the right-hand side with Peter tracking his run.

But Crowny didn't pass. He shot instead. It flew straight – but missed the post by a whisker.

Bradders, who had dived in a hopeless attempt to reach the shot, watched in horror as the ball smashed into the sport centre's wall and flew straight back at him.

The keeper couldn't move out of the way quickly enough.

It struck him and bounced towards the empty net ... until Harry raced in and hacked the ball off the goal line.

The ref blew immediately. Penalty.

Charlie groaned. He knew it wasn't Harry's fault – these things can happen in a match.

But he was worried about what the others would say. After all, it was his decision to call his brother to help them out.

Only goalkeepers are allowed inside the semi-circles surrounding five-a-side goals – and Harry had broken that rule.

Harry looked like he might cry.

Annie placed a hand on his shoulder and pulled the boy to her.

Cage patted the ref on the back as he took the ball and placed it on the spot.

Charlie could see Bradders' face scrunched up with concentration.

Unfortunately, one of the girls on the sidelines had seen the unusual expression too.

She squealed: "Look at him! Look! Look! Look at the goalkeeper. The keeper's crying!"

She pointed in Bradders' direction before the rest of The Page Boys burst into hysterical laugher.

"Keeper's crying!

"Keeper's crying!
"Keeper's crying!"

The chant rang around the old hall.

Bradders' eyes flicked away from the ball towards the rowdy crowd next to him.

He doubled his concentration. It only made them worse.

"Keeper's crying!
"Keeper's crying!"

The chants soon turned to cheers as Cage coolly slotted home the penalty. Bradders didn't even move.

Charlie resumed kick-off duties and won the ball, mainly because Crowny didn't even attempt to win it this time.

Charlie knocked the ball backwards to Peter as both he and Harry began to move up the pitch.

It was a mistake. After pretending to be not interested, Crowny suddenly stormed forward covering the ground between him and Peter in a couple of bounds.

"Keeper's crying!
"Keeper's crying!"

Peter, caught out by the sudden pressure, was caught in two minds. A split second too late, he decided to hoof the ball clear.

Crowny made a tiny tug on his shirt and put Peter off balance.

So, instead of whacking the ball clear, he did an air shot and left the ball behind.

There was no time for mickey-taking or mockery. Annie slid desperately to try to stop the inevitable but it was too late.

Crowny simply stepped over Peter and blasted past the ball around the stunned Bradders into the top corner.

Both arms in the air, The Page Boys' star man jumped over the bench into the celebrating masses behind their bench.

He was soon joined by the rest of the team.

"Keeper's crying!
"Keeper's crying!
"Keeper's crying!"

4–0.

The final whistle blew and the You Know The Score team trooped out of the hall with the catcalls and gloating ringing in their ears.

7. ALL CHANGE

Charlie and the team collapsed in a small circle in the middle of the function room upstairs.

They felt shattered even though it had only been a four-minute game.

Bradders tried to fight back the tears.

"I knew it! I knew I'd score an own goal. My dream has finally come true!"

He flung down the gloves in rage.

Charlie bit his lip and replied gently. "Gary, you didn't score an own goal. Remember? Harry cleared it in time."

The stand-in goalkeeper looked stunned for a second.

Then he continued: "Yeah … I guess you're right … thanks, Harry … it is just … that was really embarrassing.

"I mean, all those people were laughing at me. Why were they picking on me? What have I ever done to them?"

Joe placed a hand on his shoulder.

"Ignore them, Bradders. They're idiots.

"Crowny thinks he's the big man but, if he was so great at football, he'd be playing under-18s, wouldn't he?"

Bradders shook his head and took a long slurp from his water bottle.

"Perhaps you are right.

"I don't know.

"Those girls are …"

"…awful, yes, we know," said Annie as she finished his sentence.

"But Joe's right – we have all got to ignore them."

The doors burst open.

Laughter and chanting filled the air as the victorious Page Boys team and their fans swept into the room.

They had taken over one of the far corners of the large room but, despite the distance, they still made a right racket.

Chants of "Keeper's crying" and "Football Boy Blunder" kept ringing out followed by crazy bouts of giggles.

Harry sat there with his mouth wide open.

"I never … thought it would be like this.

"I'm sorry for giving away the penalty – I totally forgot about not going into the area."

Peter put an arm around him.

"You've got nothing to apologise for, sunshine.

"It's not your fault they're idiots.

"And, besides, all of us had a stinker."

Harry offered a smile of thanks.

He began to reply but Joe got there first.

"Peter is right, Harry. None of this is your fault.

"It's mine."

The gang looked at him.

Joe hadn't even been playing.

How could this possibly be his fault?

No-one spoke.

They all just looked at Joe as he stood up and began to strip off.

He had a Blues top on underneath his tracksuit and bent down to scoop up the gloves Bradders had tossed aside.

"I should never have simply stood aside and let my friends down.

"I'll be the goalkeeper from now on."

Annie's eyes widened as she stood up.

"Joe, you can't! You are not allowed to, remember?

"What would United say if they found out that one of their star academy players was playing here?"

Joe pulled a face.

"You are only young once. I got noticed by United because I played youth football and it wasn't so bad then, was it?

"I will not sit there and watch my friends – and their little brothers – have the mickey taken out of them. What kind of friend would I be if I was happy with that?

"In fact, what kind of person would I be?

"If United somehow hear about this and get rid of me because I stuck up for my friends, then good riddance to them.

"It would be fairly obvious that they're not the right club for me.

"Football is important, of course, but it's nothing next to you guys."

One look at Joe's face told Charlie not to argue.

He had seen that expression before – it was pointless to protest.

Joe's mind was made up.

"Well said, Mr Foster."

Charlie's dad Liam spoke softly but they still jumped.

No-one had seen him approach. Liam towered over them all.

"Right, now Joe has made up his mind, you are going to need a manager.

"I guess that's me."

Again, no-one said a word.

Charlie noticed smiles creep over the faces of Peter and Joe – they knew that Liam Fry knew his football.

"Okay. We're on again ten minutes … against Melloway Men.

"Joe will play in goal, Annie in defence, Peter and Bradders in midfield and Charlie up front.

"Everyone understand?"

Liam's eyes swept the team in front of him.

His gaze stopped on Harry, who looked like he might cry at any second.

The burly builder picked up his youngest boy.

"And you, Harry lad, are going to be our team's super sub. There's still going to be loads of football for you this afternoon, my boy."

8. PESKY BLINDERS

Charlie was first through the old wooden doors on to the pitch.

The Boy Wonder raced towards the far goal as he enjoyed the briefest of moments of being alone on the pitch.

Seconds later it was over.

Joe surged past him and was soon busy dragging the tatty old mat into the right position in front of his goal.

Peter, Bradders and Annie joined Charlie.

Crowny's team had just finished their second match and the noise slowly began to die down as they made their way up the stairs.

The Page Boys had just won 6–0 against OSF, the other team in their group.

The win was actually a good thing for Charlie's team.

The top two teams in the group stage went through.

OSF and Melloway Men drew 1–1 in the group's first match so had one point each.

If You Know The Score could win the next two matches, then they would squeak through to the next round.

But first they had to beat Melloway Men: a team that boasted the Blinder twins, a pair of decent footballers who were a couple of years older than Charlie but well known throughout Crickledon.

Darren Blinder was quick like a greyhound but the size of a small wrestler.

His wavy brown hair and permanent suntan made him a hit with the girls.

Phil was even bigger, stronger and better at football than his brother.

He was a highly rated goalkeeper, who had spent years training with some of the best 'keeping coaches in the country.

The Blinder brothers were outstanding players.

And right from the kick-off, the Melloway Men went for the win.

Like Charlie's team, they knew this was a must-win game, particularly with The Page Boys being their final game.

Darren was everywhere on the pitch.

He ducked and weaved around with fancy footwork.

The Melloway Men were clever: they used the walls to pass the ball around the opposition and left Annie and Peter chasing shadows.

It was one-way traffic.

Charlie couldn't get involved in the game and, slowly but surely, Peter and Bradders got pushed back too.

In the Melloway goal, Phil had barely touched the ball.

But it had been a different story at the end of the pitch.

Joe had been in the thick of the action.

He had pushed one effort on to the post and slid out to the edge of his area to intercept a dangerous cross.

Yet the score remained 0–0.

By half-time Charlie was feeling exhausted and, yet again, he had hardly touched the ball.

The magic target continued to harmlessly float around his eyesight – but he had not used it once today.

It was no surprise when his dad sent on Harry in his place for the second half.

For once, Charlie did not argue.

"Well played, son."

Charlie knew his dad was only being kind. He had been rubbish but the Boy Wonder felt too tired to care.

Indoor football was relentless and he needed a breather.

Besides he was happy his brother would get another chance – after the nightmare against The Page Boys.

"Come on You Know The Score!" Joe bellowed as he switched ends and clapped his gloves together with a thud.

Darren won the kick-off again and moments later sent a left-foot screamer in the direction of Joe's goal.

Joe pushed it wide but it hit the wall at pace and bounced clear of his area before he could manage to gather it.

Peter raced towards the ball with two Melloway players close behind. He could not turn without losing possession.

He had one option and blasted the ball as hard as he could … back towards his own goal.

It flashed past a shocked Joe for a second time in a few seconds and rebounded off the brickwork with a loud thud.

It rocketed past Peter and the players surrounding him. It glanced off the side wall too, which took it past Darren's outstretched leg.

The extra deflection caught everyone off guard.

Apart from one person.

Harry Fry had read where the ball would land and was waiting for it midway inside the Melloway half.

He was on his own.

The little striker turned with the confidence of a Premier League player and, without even looking up, slotted the ball low into the bottom corner of the net.

GOAL!

The Boy Wonder watched with delight as his brother wheeled away in celebration with both of his arms in the air.

"Get in!"

Charlie could not hide his own excitement. His little brother was going to be some player in a few years' time.

Phil looked down at the ball tangled in the net with amazement.

He had not even dived.

The littlest player in the tournament had got Charlie's team up and running.

9. MAKE OR BREAK

Harry ran to his dad, who pulled him into a huge bear hug.

They were soon joined by Charlie and the rest of the team, who slapped Harry on the back for such a cool finish.

Liam Fry peeled his son away and looked sternly at the team.

"Remember: you must concentrate.

"They will throw everything at us now."

Annie nodded.

"Come on, boys.

"There's still a match to win."

The others murmured in agreement.

The Melloway Men were waiting for kick-off with a shocked look on their faces.

Darren Blinder gave Harry a small pat on the back as the boy jogged past.

"Well done, kid."

Harry blushed but Charlie could see his brother puff his chest out with pride as Peter went up for the kick-off.

When the game restarted, the Melloway Men threw everything into finding the equaliser that would keep them in the competition.

Joe, as usual, was unruffled.

He threw himself around like a man possessed, utterly determined not to concede an equaliser.

Charlie watched from the sidelines in awe.

The others were working hard, closing down and harassing the Melloway Men – but Joe was the difference.

The ball seemed to always be pulled in his direction.

And when Darren did finally beat him with a typical thunderbolt, the crossbar came to You Know The Score's rescue.

With 10 seconds to go and the ball with Melloway keeper Phil Blinder, it looked like Harry's super finish and Joe's heroics had won the game.

Then disaster struck.

Without even looking up, Phil smashed the ball forward.

It went like a rocket towards You Know The Score's goal.

Joe sensed the danger and began to move as the low shot flew through the crowded midfield area.

He dropped to his knees to get his full weight behind it … and then Annie threw out a leg in a desperate attempt to block the ball.

It was the worst thing that could have happened.

The ball sliced off Annie's outstretched foot and completely changed direction.

It left Joe wrong-footed.

And he could only watch helplessly as the ball – now travelling far slower – spun beyond the stretch of his right hand and trickled into the net.

1–1.

Phil Blinder threw up his arms in delight as the ref blew the final whistle. Within seconds, the rest of the Melloway team jumped on him.

It was a draw but it felt like another defeat for You Know The Score.

After a quick round of handshakes, the teams headed upstairs to wait for the final round of matches.

You Know The Score sat quietly.

They had been so close.

Liam didn't let them mull over the draw for long.

"Well played, team."

Peter didn't hold back.

"Are you kidding? We just threw it away."

Liam rubbed a big hand over the stubble on his chin as he considered Peter's comment.

"Yes, we were close. But that was a freak goal at the end.

"But look at it this way: you've managed to get all of your bad luck out of the way in the first two games.

"And you're still right in this competition.

"If The Page Boys beat Melloway Men, which is pretty likely, then a win will take us through to the semis.

"And once you get into the knockout stages of a competition, anything can happen.

"Of course, the same applies to OSF – they only need a win too and they will be thinking exactly the same as us.

"But I've got a feeling we'll see them off.

"Our luck is about to change."

10. TURNAROUND

Liam Fry had been right.

The Page Boys hammered the Melloway Men 4-1 – with Crowny bagging a hat-trick as they topped the group.

And You Know The Score comfortably swept aside OSF with ease to snatch second place and seal a spot in the semi-finals.

It was an easy 2-0 victory for Charlie's team.

The Boy Wonder opened the scoring inside the first 30 seconds.

One of the OSF defenders did not read Bradders' clever pass off the wall and got her body in a pickle as she tried to clear it.

This allowed the ball to invitingly bounce into Charlie's path.

It was all he needed – a sniff of a chance.

With the blink of an eye, the magic target had sprung into life and locked on to the bottom corner of the OSF goal.

A heartbeat later it flashed green – and Charlie struck the ball beautifully with the outside of his right foot.

It skimmed over the well-worn floor and beyond the despairing dive of the young OSF goalkeeper.

Boom!

One chance. One opportunity to use the magic target. One goal.

The Boy Wonder was back.

Annie had wrapped up the scoring after Harry, who had replaced Bradders for the second half, skipped past a tackle and passed across the goal for a simple tap-in.

Job done.

You Know The Score were now up and running – but the five-a-side competition was about to get serious.

Charlie stood in front of the double doors at the top of the sport centre's stairs, looking at the semi-final fixtures:

Semi-Final One: The Page Boys v Dabbing It
Semi-Final Two: Hopless United v You Know The Score.

Annie stood beside him.

"Well, at least we're not playing Crowny's mob.

"That's one thing to be grateful for."

Charlie smiled weakly.

The first semi-final was already under way.

They would be playing next.

"Yeah, you're right ... except...."

His voice tailed off.

As usual, Annie knew exactly what he was thinking.

"Wrecka."

Charlie nodded.

The Hall Park Magpies captain was one of their great friends – yet today he would be lining up against them.

That was not good. Wrecka was a hell of a player.

He was one of those defenders that never gave you a moment, always snapping at attackers' ankles or tugging at a shirt to keep them off balance.

Annie took his hand.

"Come on, your dad is calling us."

Charlie hadn't heard his dad's calls.

The room had begun to empty now that teams were getting knocked out.

Some stayed – like the Blinder brothers – to watch the final but many of the players had left already.

Charlie and Annie jogged over to the rest of the team.

Liam Fry gathered them into a tight circle.

"Right, this is it.

"Remember how good we are. We are a proper team.

"You've not even played well yet.

"Football is all about rhythm.

"And we are the ones on a roll. This competition is ours."

Joe spoke up for the team.

"We shouldn't underestimate this lot though. They're a really good team – with decent players, particularly Wrecka."

Liam nodded in agreement.

"No-one is going to underestimate them but, believe me, there is nobody who is going to want to face you lot. Get out there and show them exactly why you're the team to be feared."

A door slammed open.

Seconds later, chanting filled the air.

"Crowny! Crowny! Crowny!"

The Page Boys had just booked their place in the final.

11. OLD FRIENDS

"Hopless?"

Wrecka threw his head back and laughed loudly as he stood on the pitch with Peter and Charlie.

The big defender grinned: "I know. That's what you get when you send that muppet to fill in the team name at the start of the competition."

He flicked his eyes in the direction of the Hopless goalkeeper, who had been warming up intensely ever since they had wandered into the hall.

Rick Tightline wore a bright pink goalkeeper jersey, yellow shorts and green trainers. He barely had a hair out of place.

Tightline perhaps could not spell very well but he was friendly enough.

He occasionally joined Charlie and the rest of the gang down at The Rec for a summer evening kickabout.

He was remarkable in one sense – he had all of the latest goalkeeper kit – but he rarely made a save. No-one had ever seen him get dirty, and he never stopped moaning.

If there was a complaint to be made, Tightline would almost certainly be the person behind it.

Wrecka chuckled: "We were supposed to be 'Hopeless United'.

"But Rick somehow managed to spell it wrong so we've been called 'Hopless United' ever since.

"Everyone has found it hilarious – apart from him.

"He has spent most of the afternoon moaning at the officials to change it but they think it's funny too so he's had no luck."

Tightline saw the boys looking over and raised a hand in their direction before getting back to his stretching routine.

And he wasn't the only friendly face on Wrecka's team.

They also had Bim, the Choldington Weavers striker who had scored against Hall Park Magpies earlier in the season.

With the ball not being allowed to go over head height, the gangly striker couldn't use his height this time to beat them.

Nonetheless Annie and Bradders would have their hands full. Bim was a quality player.

Apart from the goalkeepers, the teams were equally matched.

Charlie shot out a hand to Wrecka.

"May the best team win."

Wrecka high-fived his football buddy and then did the same to Peter. "Good luck Boy Wonder."

Peter went up for the kick-off against Bim.

The bigger boy won the challenge and sent the ball back to Wrecka, who smashed the ball forward with gusto.

It went straight through to Joe, who held on to the ball for a couple of seconds and then rolled it out to Annie.

Crash!

Bim's shoulder ploughed into Annie and sent her straight into the brick wall.

Annie yelped and collapsed in a heap.

"Ref!" Peter shouted.

To everyone's amazement, the ref waved play on.

Bim rolled the ball away from Annie, who was helpless on the floor, and prepared to shoot.

As he did so, Bradders flung himself in the way with a magnificent slide tackle, which took the ball and a shocked Bim with him.

The ball squirmed away towards Joe again as the pair of boys tried to untangle themselves in the corner of the pitch.

Liam Fry was on his feet, clapping.

"Great tackle, Bradders lad! Come on You Know The Score, let's get started," he bellowed from behind the wooden bench.

But the game continued in the same vein.

The blue shirts of You Know The Score tried to pass their way up the pitch but Wrecka stopped everything.

Tightline had only had one save to make – a limp pea-roller along the floor from Annie, which he dramatically stopped like it was a top-corner thunderbolt.

From the start, Hopless's tactic was clear: get the ball up the pitch towards Bim as quickly as possible. And it was working.

Peter and Charlie were being bypassed.

Wrecka kept making wonderful interceptions every time the ball came towards them and booted it back towards Joe's goal.

Bradders and Annie were sweating as the ref's whistle blew for half-time. There was only one team that was going to win this – unless something changed quickly.

12. BROTHERS

As the teams switched ends, Charlie's dad summoned You Know The Score over for a quick pep talk.

"Annie, are you okay? That looked a nasty tackle."

Annie appeared to be a little wobbly but replied: "I'm fine."

Liam watched her with concern for a moment before looking around the rest of the team.

"This is close. They're a decent team with clever tactics."

Everyone nodded. They did not have much to say – they were all busy drinking water or trying to catch their breath.

"It's time for us to make a change.

"Peter, you're coming off for Harry this time."

"What?" Charlie, Annie and Bradders all answered at the same time.

To Charlie's surprise though, Peter did not argue. He simply nodded and stepped over the wooden bench to take a seat.

"Wrecka knows you all too well. He knows what you're going to do. He knows that Charlie only needs a sight of the goal to score. So he's stopping you having the ball near the goal.

"As a result, we need to be clever too. Harry, you go up top on your own. Wrecka has never seen you play before – it will make him hesitate."

Joe rubbed his chin, deep in thought: "Yeah, I think I understand.

"With Harry on, we can drop Charlie into the midfield away from Wrecka.

"He can pick the ball up deep and either be able to shoot – or play Harry in because he's the only one who knows how Harry plays."

Liam slapped Joe on the back.

"Bingo, Mr Foster! Let's give them something different to worry about. It's time we gave that goalkeeper a few headaches."

You Know The Score's players bounced back into their positions with a new confidence.

Charlie could see Wrecka looking suspiciously at Harry.

They had been friends for a long time but he could not remember Wrecka ever facing his little brother – either at The Rec or in his back garden.

He smiled to himself. His brother was something special – when he wasn't being really annoying, of course.

The ref blew the whistle and dropped the ball.

A split-second later Harry had nipped in to swipe it away from a shocked-looking Bim.

The youngster played it straight back to Charlie. The Boy Wonder wasn't even on the halfway line but it did not matter.

His target almost instantly flicked on to the Hopless goal, flashed green and Charlie pulled the trigger.

The target had not been in the corner but it didn't matter.

Charlie knew it was important to move everyone up the pitch.

The ball whistled easily past the Hopless players – Wrecka had followed Harry towards the left side of the pitch and, for once, wasn't there to block the shot.

Tightline's eyes widened as the ball zoomed towards him.

He flung a padded glove at the ball and forced it on to the bar.

The ball ricocheted back towards Wrecka, who had desperately dashed back towards his own goal, met the ball with his head on the edge of the area.

But he had misjudged the power of the shot. The ball cannoned off Wrecka's head and went straight into the air.

"FOUL!"

Every member of You Know The Score threw their hands up in the air at the same time.

Charlie's dad and Peter were screaming from the bench too.

The ref looked at the ball high in the air and blew his whistle.

"That is a free-kick to the blues. The ball clearly went over head height."

Hands on his head, Wrecka could not believe his mistake.

The ref placed the ball on the edge of the area … and told the Hopless players there was no room for a wall – unless they wanted to give away a penalty.

Annie grabbed the ball. They had worked on several free-kick routines throughout the summer.

Charlie scooted to the other side of the pitch.

He knew exactly what she had planned but the others had not been part of their park practice sessions.

Before he could say a word, Annie had grabbed them. They nodded as Annie spoke quickly, turned and stood directly over the ball.

"Ref! I can't see!"

Tightline, as usual, was whining. With Bradders and Harry standing in the way, the keeper's vision was blocked.

The ref shook his head.

"That's not my problem. They are perfectly entitled to stand over it – it's fine as long as none of them take a step into your penalty area, of course."

Tightline continued to grumble but not loud enough for the ref to hear.

Making sure that everyone was watching, Bradders looked in Charlie's direction and gave a thumbs-up.

Wrecka spotted the signal straight away and moved a step closer to Charlie.

He whispered: "I know this is coming straight to you, Boy Wonder. You forget that I train with you every week! Why on earth wouldn't you be taking it? You think you can fool everyone – but not me."

Charlie grinned but said nothing in response.

The ref blew his whistle again.

"Charlie!"

Annie shouted as she began her run up.

Charlie moved … but ran away from the Hopless goal.

The Hopless players stopped in their tracks, confused by the opposition's unexpected movements.

When Annie was a step away from the ball, Bradders and Harry calmly stepped to the side.

Unable to see the ball, Tightline had been watching Charlie.

He turned back too late. He did not move a muscle as Annie calmly side-footed the ball into the far corner of the net.

GOAL!

"YES!" Annie punched the air and was soon swamped by the rest of the team. Joe scampered down the pitch to celebrate too.

"I can't believe it worked!"

Charlie shook his head in amazement too.

All those hours playing on The Rec had finally paid off.

One of the free-kick routines had actually paid off.

Now they just had to hang on – and a rematch with Crowny would await them.

13. NERVES

Liam Fry stood in front of the jubilant You Know The Score team.

The Page Boys and their fans were already heading down the stairs to get into the hall first.

That suited You Know The Score.

The 2–0 victory over Hopless only finished a couple of minutes ago and the team needed a breather.

Joe had – as usual – performed miracles in goal to keep the ball out of the net.

With only seconds remaining at the end of pulsating semi-final, a loose ball had fallen to Charlie with Wrecka close behind.

Charlie did not hesitate.

He simply belted the ball down the pitch as hard as he could.

The Boy Wonder hoped the clearance would encourage the ref to blow for full-time.

But instead the ball found its way to an unmarked Harry, who had a clear run on goal.

Harry did not hesitate. He ignored Tightline's pathetic attempt to put him off and calmly side-footed the ball past the hapless keeper into the net.

As the ball nestled into the net, the ref blew for full-time.

They had done it.

The organisers had given You Know The Score a five-minute break before the final kicked off.

Charlie and the gang were buzzing.

After they struggled to get started, the team had come from nowhere to claim a place in the final.

Now they faced Simon Crown and the rest of The Page Boys again.

Crowny's gang seemed to be delighted to be facing Charlie's team again.

Chants of "One Boy Blunder!" and "Keeper's crying!" echoed around the centre as the final members of the gang sauntered past.

Charlie's dad waited for the racket to die down before he spoke.

He smiled as the words came out: "You lot are something else.

"I am so proud today … of all of you."

Liam crouched down and dropped his voice so no-one could overhear them.

"This is it. This is what we've been waiting for. Remember what happened in that awful first game … and learn from it.

"We need to stick together. Hunt the ball in packs.

"Run until you cannot run any more. We will sub regularly to keep our legs as fresh as possible. Go out there and give absolutely everything. If they win, fair enough, but at least you'll give them a real game this time."

He stood up again and rubbed his back.

"I'm too old for this. Harry, you're the first sub.

"Come on, let's go down there first and wait for the best team in this competition to join us."

Harry gave the rest of the team a thumbs up.

He was beaming with joy.

Charlie knew today had been like a dream for him.

As Liam and Harry disappeared down the stairs, several figures approached the team from the other side of the room.

It was Wrecka, Tightline and the Blinder brothers who stood above them.

Wrecka grinned: "Just so you know: they may have all the support down there … but everyone up here is right behind you lot."

Phil added: "Yeah, we're all sick of the boasting and gloating.

"It's time their run ended. You guys can do it – especially with the Boy Wonder in your ranks."

Charlie squirmed a little. His little brother had played better than him so far. Indoor football gave him so much less time to use his target. He gritted his teeth. This was it.

And he agreed with Blinder – someone had to stop Crowny at some point.

Why couldn't they do it?

Peter had been quiet since he had been subbed in the last match.

He looked tired – and seemed to be missing his usual bags of energy.

Now though he sprung to his feet.

"Thanks lads. Don't worry about us. I've got no intention of leaving here as a runner-up."

14. THE FINAL

The Page Boys had won the Crickledon Sports Centre five-a-side competition ever since Charlie and the gang had been going.

Most of them were now nearly too old to play.

This would be the last one for most of the all-conquering team – but they didn't want to let their long-held title slip away in the final.

Jeers and songs greeted Charlie and the gang as they entered the hall.

"There's only one Boy Blunder! One Boy Blunder, one Boy Blunder...."

Joe reached the other end of the pitch and placed his water bottle inside the tatty goal net.

A new chant started.

"Keeper's crying! Keeper's crying! Keeper's crying!"

The song seemed out of place now.

First, Bradders was not crying and, secondly, he was not even playing in goal this time.

Joe looked up at the gaggle of gloating boys and girls in the far corner.

He gave them a sarcastic salute and went to back to concentrating on the match.

The catcalling stopped.

But now there was new sound – a loud banging was coming from the windows overlooking the pitch.

Charlie looked up to find the source of the din.

Wrecka, the Blinder brothers and most of their teammates were standing up bashing on the windows.

The Boy Wonder smiled. It was obvious who they were cheering for.

They would get into trouble for that – but their support made him stick his chest out.

You could not show fear against this lot. They were ready.

The ref held the ball in his hand ready for the kick-off.

Peter eased Charlie out of the way.

"Let me have this one."

Charlie shrugged.

Peter still did not look too well but something in his tone told

Charlie not to argue.

Charlie stepped backwards as Crowny sauntered towards the drop ball spot.

"Has the Boy Wonder chickened out again?

"To be honest that's not a surprise – he knows it's a lost cause."

The ref ignored Crowny.

"Right, this is the final so the match is two and a half minutes each way.

"If the scores are equal at the final whistle, it is penalties.

"Everyone understand?"

The ref did not wait for a response.

He dropped the ball and retreated out of the way.

Peter did not hesitate.

His foot shot out and smashed straight into Crowny's thigh.

He was nowhere near the ball.

The older boy collapsed in agony as the ball remained untouched in the small centre circle.

Peter stood over him: "Not so clever now, are you?"

Bang! Bang! Bang!

Charlie thought the upstairs windows were going to cave in.

This seemed to spur Crowny into life.

Forgetting the pain in his leg, he jumped to his feet and pushed Peter in the chest: "Who do you think you are, Titch?"

Within seconds, Bradders had waded in to the shoving match as well as several Page Boys players.

The ref blew his whistle several times as he tried to regain control.

"Right, that is a free kick to Page Boys.

"Blue shirt, calm down. Let's have no more of that, shall we?"

Crowny snatched the ball and dumped it down on exactly the same spot where the kick-off happened.

Peter stood a couple of metres away with his hands out in front of him.

Crowny sneered: "This is going to hurt – a nice little bit of pay back for that foul, you loser."

Peter winked back at him.

Crowny looked like he might explode.

He ran full steam towards the ball and ignored his teammates' pleas for a quick pass.

A moment later he blasted the ball straight at Peter, who was ready.

He dropped to his knees and rolled on to his stomach in the flash of an eye.

Instead of hitting the opposition player, the ball flew upwards into the netting that stretched across the roof.

The ref blew his whistle.

"That is quite obviously over head height.

"Free kick to You Know The Score."

Joe threw the ball back to the ref, who caught it and replaced it on the same spot where the first free-kick had been taken.

Peter bounced back to his feet with a grin and moved away from the ball.

"Wow. That was impressive ... easily the worst free kick I've ever seen."

Crowny stepped in Peter's direction.

His temper was out of control – he had forgotten about the football match.

It was the chance Charlie needed.

With Crowny distracted and no-one else bothering to block his line of sight, he zoned the target under The Page Boys crossbar.

Once it locked into place, he let the magic target flash green and smashed the shot with everything he had.

Crowny wasn't even looking at the ball when Charlie shot sweetly with his right foot.

It flashed towards the goal.

The Page Boys goalkeeper – who was used to hardly making any saves – barely moved.

It flew past his left hand, crashed off the underside of the bar and hit the back of the net.

GOAL!

Charlie threw his arms up in the air.

The banging on the upstairs windows started again.

It was now louder than ever.

You Know The Score had the lead.

15. EVERY OUNCE OF EFFORT

The two teams were huddled at opposite ends of the pitch.

It was half-time and the score remained 1–0.

Liam Fry was red-faced with excitement.

Charlie rarely saw his dad get so excited – but today was different.

"That was brilliant, just brilliant!"

Led by Peter, they had hassled and harried The Page Boys throughout the whole first half.

It had been hard work, but they were still in front and that was all that mattered.

Peter, though, did not look well.

He had turned ghostly white and was sitting slumped down behind the bench.

"Something is wrong.

"In fact, I feel awful.

"I can't play in the second half."

Everyone else looked at him.

Peter, always so determined and spirited, was hardly ever ill.

He must have been feeling bad for a while yet had given everything to try to beat Crowny's mob.

And his little wind-up routine had worked a treat.

But now he was paying the penalty.

Liam rubbed his chin.

"Are you sure you can't play on, Belly?"

Peter stared at his feet. He looked like he might vomit at any second. There was no chance he could play.

Charlie could see his dad's mind begin to whir.

It was obvious Liam Fry was reluctant to pitch Harry against the far bigger and ultra-aggressive Page Boys again.

But with Peter too ill to continue, there was no other option.

"Ok, Peter. You rest up. Harry, you're on. Go up top and chase down everything."

Harry grinned and began to pull off his tracksuit bottoms.

He didn't seem scared in the slightest.

Liam turned to the rest of the team.

"They're going to come at you with all guns blazing. Stay strong. Don't be scared. Keep going – and if you get the chance, Charlie, pinch another one."

You Know The Score bounced back to the pitch with Liam's words ringing in their eyes.

They were two and a half minutes from winning the Crickledon Under-14s Five-a-Side tournament for the first time.

But Charlie's dad had been right: The Page Boys had no intention of simply giving up the title they had held for years.

From the kick-off, The Page Boys surged forward in search of the equaliser.

Harry barely got a kick as the rest of the team got deeper and deeper against the tides of Page Boys attacks.

But Charlie, Annie and Bradders gave as good as they got.

They refused to be bullied or intimidated – with Bradders even squishing Ryan Cage against the sport centre wall with a hefty tackle.

And when they did break through, Joe was there to stop anything.

One minute to go and The Page Boys fans had begun to look concerned.

Thirty seconds later and the players started to panic as time ticked down.

And then it happened.

In a last desperate attack, Crowny punted the ball in the direction of Joe's goal.

He struck it sweetly.

The ball crashed off the bar into the net as Joe clutched at thin air.

"Boom! No-one beats us!"

Crowny yelled as he celebrated in front of Charlie's dad and a sick-looking Peter.

He was swamped by his teammates and most of The Page Boys supporters, who had excitedly invaded the pitch.

No-one was banging on windows upstairs now.

Joe stayed on his knees. The rest of You Know The Score were exhausted and could barely stand up. They had given everything.

The ref blew the full-time whistle while the celebrations were still going on.

The Crickledon Under-14s Five-a-Side tournament would be settled by a penalty shootout.

16. ONE KICK

The ref flipped the coin.

"Heads it is."

Crowny clenched his fist in celebration.

"Yes."

The ref looked at him.

"Do you want to go first or second?"

Crowny knew the answer without asking his teammates.

"We'll go first."

Charlie shrugged. He had expected that decision.

They wanted to score first and pile pressure on the younger team.

Joe stepped into the goalmouth and ignored the usual chanting from Page Boys supporters.

One of the big Page Boys defenders stepped forward and placed the ball on the edge of the area.

Two steps back and he was ready. He looked at the referee who blew the whistle. The defender strolled forward and toe-punted the ball towards the corner.

As quick as a flash, Joe dived to his right. His gloved hand reached the ball and sent it wide of the post.

Miss!

Bang! Bang! Bang! For the first time in ages, the upstairs windows began to rattle again.

The defender put his head in his hands as he walked back to the silent fans of The Page Boys. They could not believe it.

Annie was first penalty taker for You Know The Score.

Super confident, she plonked the ball down and waited for the whistle.

The ref blew. Four steps and....

Annie hit it so sweetly.

It went like a rocket along the floor ... but straight into the gut of the shocked goalkeeper.

He never moved an inch and seemed winded by the sheer power of the shot. Nonetheless, the ball stayed out. The Page Boys bench erupted while You Know The Score groaned with disappointment.

0–0.

Ryan Cage was next up for The Page Boys.

As he placed the ball, Charlie turned to his dad.

"Dad, I'll take the next one. Swap me with Harry."

Harry was due to take the next penalty, then Bradders with Charlie taking the final one.

Liam raised his eyebrows. "Why?"

Cage waited for the whistle and calmly slotted the ball past Joe's outstretched arm into the bottom left corner.

1–0.

Huge cheers from The Page Boys end.

Charlie replied: "We need to get a goal on the board.

"If we don't, this shootout could be over before I even get to take one."

Charlie did not wait for an answer. It was the right thing to do.

He grabbed the ball and placed it on the spot. No run-up was needed.

A blink of his eye and the target locked on to the corner – exactly where Cagey had scored.

The whistle blew. The target locked green and Charlie laced the ball into the corner.

Again the keeper didn't move – but he did not get lucky for a second time.

1–1!

The pounding on the windows started again as Charlie returned to the rest of the team with a huge smile on his face.

One of The Page Boys midfielders was next up.

He strode up and side-footed the ball calmly towards the opposite corner that Charlie had scored in.

But he had hit it too softly.

Joe's outstretched leg stopped the ball in its tracks.

Miss!

"YESSS!"

Every member of You Know The Score was up cheering together – even an exhausted Peter was on his feet.

Bradders marched up full of determination.

"Keeper's crying! Keeper's crying! Keeper's crying!"

Charlie could see a shadow of doubt across Bradders' face as he paced away from the ball.

Immediately he knew what was going to happen.

Bradders ran full pelt at the ball – too fast.

He crashed into the shot and sent the ball flying past the post. Miss!

The Page Boys team and fans burst into laughter. It was an awful shot and poor Bradders looked gutted as he walked back to the team. He dropped down on to the bench unable to look at anyone.

Joe raced to take his place in goal for the final time.

The singing started again.

"Keeper's crying! Keeper's crying!"

Crowny swaggered up and pointed.

"I'm going for that corner, goalie."

He smirked and took two paces back. The ref blew.

Crowny began his run-up ... and then stopped.

The unexpected shimmy fooled Joe, who had guessed the ball was going to his right and fell to the ground helplessly.

With a grin, Crowny hammered the ball towards the top corner in the opposition direction to the way Joe had dived.

Crash. The ball struck the bar and rocketed back out again. Miss!

Crowny's mouth fell open as the banging began again. The centre's upstairs windows sounded as if they would break at any moment.

Joe turned and put his finger to his lips towards the silent Page Boys fans.

Crowny had missed. It was still 1–1. Only one kick remained.

Harry Fry.

"Concentrate on the ball. Nothing else."

Liam Fry whispered to his youngest son as he began the long walk to the penalty spot.

The Page Boys goalkeeper was jumping around to try to put Harry off. Their fans were also singing some silly chant too.

Harry ignored everything. He followed his dad's advice. Charlie knew where Harry would put it.

His favourite shot was always across the goalkeeper, low and to the right of the keeper.

Everything stopped. They all waited for the ref to blow his whistle. The singing died off. The banging of the windows ceased.

The keeper crouched as he waited for the whistle.

Charlie could see Harry bite his lip with nerves.

"Come on!" Charlie murmured to himself. He felt more nervous watching his brother than taking his own penalty.

Finally the ref blew.

Harry took three steps and struck the shot cleanly – exactly where Charlie had predicted.

The goalkeeper dived but could not reach the ball.

It hit the inside of the post and rebounded into the net.

GOAL!

Harry Fry – the youngest player in the competition – had scored the deciding penalty to win the trophy.

"YEESSSS!"

Harry jumped in the air as the rest of You Know The Score leaped from the bench with joy. They had done it.

BANG! BANG! BANG!

Charlie looked up. He could see Wrecka, the Blinder brothers and Tightline all thumping the glass in celebration. Charlie gave them the thumbs-up.

When he turned around again, his brother was buried under the rest of the team who had caught up with him.

Charlie began to make his way to join them but was stopped by a hand tapping his shoulder.

Simon Crown stuck out a hand: "Well played. You deserved that today."

Charlie was lost for words but accepted the handshake.

"Thank you. It was a hell of a game."

Crowny chuckled.

"You could say that. This is the first indoor tournament we've lost in three years – and it appears we were beaten by a nipper."

It was Charlie's turn to laugh.

He was right: Harry was years younger than the rest of them.

"He'll probably end up better than any of us."

Crowny nodded his agreement and turned away, leaving Charlie to pull Harry free from the pile of bodies.

His brother beamed with excitement.

"I scored Charlie! It was just like we had always practised!

"We did it. We're the champions."

Charlie heard a laugh behind them. It was their dad.

"I'm never going to hear the end of this, am I?"

"NEVER!" shouted his boys together, and they meant it too.

Charlie Fry and the Grudge Match

1. THE CARPET

The ball bounced off the tree and rolled towards the wide concrete path that ran through the heart of Crickledon Rec.

Charlie Fry sighed and began to amble towards his prize possession.

He checked his watch. It was 6.10pm.

This was the problem with the school summer holidays.

Having six weeks off was great, of course, but it turned all normal arrangements upside down.

Charlie and his friends played at Crickledon Rec every Monday, Thursday and Sunday at 6pm. There was no need for messages or texts. Everyone knew the times because it was the same every week.

Usually there was easily enough of them to play a six-a-side game.

Trees were used as sturdy goalposts at the end where Charlie stood now.

The goal at the other end of the makeshift pitch was formed through a mixture of bikes, bags and jumpers.

There were no official markings so they never bothered with throw-ins, meaning the pitch could easily be as wide as it was long.

But that patch of grass was special. In Charlie's mind, it had hosted some of the best games ever – nothing could beat a 21-19 thriller on a Sunday evening.

However, in the school summer holidays, things changed. People went away for weeks on end. Most went on the usual sun and seaside break. Some stayed with relatives in distant counties.

Others – without the usual school routine to remind them – simply forgot.

Charlie and those who remained in Crickledon had struggled for numbers for the past couple of weeks.

Only four had turned up on Thursday, so they'd had to settle for a game of heads and volleys instead.

Today was even worse.

Charlie had got there early to make sure he did not miss anyone.

But, so far, no-one had turned up. He yawned.

They would be back soon, he knew, but by then it would be nearly the end of park football for another year.

The September nights soon got dark too quickly for a proper evening match. October was even worse.

And once those clocks went back, the park football season was finished until next March. To make matters worse, there was a large group of lads playing a couple of trees down.

Charlie thought he recognised a few of their faces but did not know their names. He was sure most of them lived on the opposite side of the town. They rarely, if ever, played at the Rec. They seemed to be a mixture of ages but they were mainly Charlie's age or older.

Absorbed in their own game, they ignored the Boy Wonder and made no effort to invite him to play or speak to him.

Charlie had frowned as soon as he had spotted them. It happened sometimes. Crickledon Rec was a popular park and it seemed like the entire town loved football at the moment.

But it was always a touch awkward when the two makeshift pitches were placed next to each other.

It didn't work well, particularly with the lack of pitch markings. Often balls would invade the other game by accident.

Still it didn't matter today – there was only one match being played and Charlie certainly wasn't part of it.

Charlie checked his watch again: 6.14pm. It was too late.

No-one else was coming today. Charlie wished his best mates Joe Foster and Peter Bell were there.

Peter had gone on holiday to Portugal yesterday while Joe was on his first-ever tour with United. They wouldn't be back in Crickledon for another week. Until then, Charlie was flying solo.

He made up his mind quickly: he would go home and practice shooting in the back garden with his little brother Harry.

It would not be a complete waste of an evening.

His magic target – which allowed him to place the ball anywhere he liked with the blink of an eye – would have to wait until tomorrow to get a proper workout.

Taking one last look at the group of strangers playing football on the Rec's neatly trimmed carpet of grass, the Boy Wonder picked up his back-pack, kept the football at his feet under close control and headed home.

Tomorrow he would try again – and was sure that the strangers would be long gone by then.

2. HOME TURF

Charlie had been wrong. The strangers had not gone anywhere.

When he turned up a day later, they were there again.

Charlie knew instantly it was the same big gang as the day before.

And this time it was worse – much worse. His heart sank.

Instead of making a pitch and using the trees as goals, they had turned the pitch sideways – so their pitch ran across all the usual pitches on the Rec.

It left Charlie and his friends nowhere to play.

The Boy Wonder dumped his bag between the trees that they usually used for a goal. Today though, if he ventured out of the goalmouth, he would step on to the strangers' pitch.

"What's going on?"

A puzzled-looking Billy Savage was approaching him.

Billy played alongside Charlie for Hall Park Magpies.

He was a quiet lad but a good player.

Charlie liked him even if Billy's hair products stunk out their changing rooms every week.

As usual, Billy's dark mop was smothered in gel and immaculately pushed forward.

Charlie smiled. At least he wasn't on his own today.

"Hey Billy, how's things?"

Billy threw his bag down alongside Charlie's backpack.

He shrugged: "Fine. Sorry, I missed yesterday – my dad's dinner wasn't ready in time. I couldn't believe he had spent all day making dinner and yet it was still late – but that's the way it goes."

Charlie clapped a hand on Billy's back. He was the same size as Charlie.

"Don't worry buddy. We'll play around them – somehow."

Billy did not look convinced. "How are we going to do that? Their pitch is huge! There's hardly any room for anyone else."

Billy spoke loudly. A couple of the strangers turned and looked at them for a moment.

"What's going on?"

Charlie knew Emma Tysoe was heading their way before he had turned around.

Blonde ponytail swinging behind her, Emma marched up to the

boys with an indignant look on her face.

Toby Grace followed a few steps behind her, panting for breath.

Charlie pulled a face: "They got here first.

"There's not much we can do. It is a public park – you can play where you want."

Emma went red in the face, which was never a good sign.

"But they are playing in the wrong direction!

"Everyone knows the rules of Crickledon Rec: you have a goal in the trees at one end and use bags at the other.

"This pitch goes across everyone else's!"

Emma spoke loudly – far louder than Billy did.

This time most of the strangers stopped and turned towards them.

Within seconds, several of the boys were heading in their direction.

"Oh no," muttered Toby, who was even smaller than Charlie.

Emma did not care.

She marched out to meet the approaching gang without a backward glance. Charlie scratched his short blonde hair and began to follow a few steps behind his friend.

"What's the problem?" The boy asked.

"You're the problem," replied Emma as her ears turned a bright shade of purple. "You're hogging all the pitches by setting up the wrong way round."

The boy smirked. "Look Blondie, we were here first. You don't own the park. Whoever gets here first gets the pick of pitches. And we have been here for ages. We want to play this way. There's loads of space over there."

He waved towards the other side of the park across the wide pathway. No-one ever played over there.

The other part of Crickledon Rec was covered in small, rolling hills – totally unsuitable for a decent game of football.

Emma shook her head: "Err, no. I don't think so. We always play here. This is our home ground."

Several more of the strangers had broken away from the game to hear the discussion. A couple of them were the same size as Charlie but most of were taller.

One shouted: "Everything alright, Trev?"

Trev held up a hand to show he had it under control. He reminded Charlie of a barrel – short and stocky.

Charlie began to feel a little nervous.

Emma appeared not to have noticed.

Trev sniggered: "Don't be so pathetic, you bunch of losers. It's a public park. We'll play where we want."

Emma wouldn't let it rest. "Why have you suddenly started turning up here? We've never seen you before."

This was true. Charlie's friends often had people joining them for a kick-about. But this bunch had never been seen at the Rec before.

The boy replied: "Yeah, we play at Moss Green, but it is out of action for the time being – so we decided to come here."

Moss Green was a small park wedged between two sets of garages on the far side of town, a minute's walk from Hall Park's stadium.

They had a couple of football goals and it was common knowledge that the park's long grass made football difficult.

Emma nodded slowly: "I remember reading something about that in the Telegraph. Aren't they putting a new play area in there?"

Toby chipped in: "Yeah, it's supposed to take two months!"

Trev nodded: "Exactly. So we need a new pitch to play on and this is perfect. We don't like using the trees as posts because there's too much dog poo under them so we turned the pitch around. So it looks like we're stuck with each other. We'll be here until September unless …."

Emma stepped forward: "Unless what?"

Trev grinned: "Unless you and your tough guys …" – he winked at Charlie, Toby and Billy – "… want to try to beat us? One match. Eight-a-side. It will be 40 minutes each way. Tomorrow night."

Emma raised an eyebrow: "And what does the winner get?"

Trev grinned: "The winner has the right to use the best pitches on the Rec. The losers find somewhere else to play. No complaints."

Emma nibbled her lip and weighed up the offer.

"We can't do tomorrow … but we could do Thursday."

Trev shrugged and stuck out a hand. "Okay, Thursday at 6pm."

Charlie could feel butterflies again. This surely wasn't worth the risk. Most of their best players were missing.

"Em …." He tried to interrupt the discussion but it was too late. "Deal!"

Emma's hand shot out and grabbed Trev's hand with a firm shake. The grudge match was on.

3. WANTED

Toby had not stopped moaning since Emma had agreed to play the Moss Green strangers in 72 hours' time.

The friends were perched on a wooden bench near to the gates at the top end of the Rec.

They turned their backs on the ongoing game of football close by.

Toby flung an arm towards their opponents: "Look over there! There are absolutely loads of them. They will have loads of subs. We hardly have enough players for a team at the moment! Have you forgotten that most of our mates are away – sunning themselves in Ibiza or Paphos or remote places I've never even heard of?

"We're going to get thrashed. Then where are we going to play?"

Charlie wanted to tell his mate to shut up and stop being negative.

The problem was Toby had a point. Emma was still red-faced – the anger had yet to disappear. So Charlie chose his words carefully.

"It will be tough but we've been up against it before, haven't we?

"I'm not sure Emma could have done anything else.

"They get here before us anyway so they will always be able to claim the pitch ahead of us. At least this way, we have a chance to get rid of them once and for all."

Emma smiled a touch, which immediately told Charlie that he had chosen the right words.

He continued: "We play the game. If we win, that will be great.

"If we lose, we'll just meet at Manor Park."

Manor Park was the home of Hall Park Magpies but it was a trek across town rather than the Rec, which was right on their doorstep.

Emma joined in: "But we're not going to lose. We're pretty good at football, remember? And we have the Football Boy Wonder."

It was Charlie's turn to go red. "Shut up."

Emma nudged his arm. "I'm serious. You're the reason why they want to play, I bet. They want to see if they can beat Crickledon's best ever footballer player."

Charlie still found his football superstar status a little odd.

Ever since a near miss with a lightning bolt had somehow transferred a target from a phone flick football app into his mind, his life had changed.

He may have cystic fibrosis and not be able to run too far but, with a flick of his eye, he could place the target anywhere – and the ball would go straight to it. All he had to do was add the power.

Only a handful of friends knew Charlie's secret and they would never tell. Deep in thought, the Boy Wonder scratched his head.

"Err no, I don't think so. I was here yesterday on my own. They could easily have invited me to play with them but they didn't."

Emma replied: "You are such a dipstick. They don't want to kick around with you! They want to BEAT you at football.

"They'll probably brag to their friends for years to come if they scrape a win against the famous Football Boy Wonder."

"Well, there's no way that's going to happen. Not a chance."

Toby was up on his feet with his hands curled into fists. The moaning had already been forgotten.

Charlie smiled. Toby was the smallest of his friends but easily the most loyal. Billy clambered to his feet too.

"We have three days to make this happen. There are four of us here so we need to find half a team and some subs. Who is about?"

Emma rubbed just above her ears with concentration.

"Annie is on holiday. She comes back on Thursday but late at night so she won't make it. She'll be so gutted."

Emma continued: "Oh, and Bradders has volunteered to spend part of the summer cleaning ambulances at the hospital.

"Actually he was volunteered by his mum. She says it will look good when he goes for jobs. I don't think he's too happy though."

Charlie pulled a face. Poor old Bradders. Parents could be really weird sometimes.

He chipped in: "So that's three Magpies players who definitely can't play. Joe and Peter are both away so let's rule them out too.

"Flem is staying with his mum's family in the countryside for the summer holidays so he won't make it."

Silence. They were seriously lacking numbers.

At this rate, they might not be able to put a team out on Thursday. Billy chirped up: "What about Mudder?"

Darren 'Mudder' Bunnell was the Magpies' goalkeeper.

Everyone shook their heads. No-one had seen Mudder in weeks.

Charlie shook his head: "No idea. I'll give him a ring. We need to get hold of the rest of the gang too – otherwise we are going to get a right thrashing."

4. COUNTDOWN

Emma sat on a bench that had been heated by the sun.

Charlie and Billy stood in front of her.

It was sweltering at the Rec with the midday sun glaring down.

All three were boiling even though they'd only worn T-shirts and shorts.

Playing football was not an option at the moment.

The big match would take place tomorrow evening and the friends had met up to discuss their team to face Moss Green.

Charlie tipped some of his water bottle over his head. The lukewarm liquid felt great as it dripped down his hair onto his top.

Water sprayed off his lips as he spoke: "So our team at the moment is the three of us, plus Toby, Mudder and Wrecka? That's not too bad."

Billy nodded: "Yeah, well done on getting Wrecka to play.

"That's a right result. We're definitely going to need him. Have you seen the size of their team?"

He was right. Half of their team – Toby, Charlie and Billy – were the shortest in their school year.

Regardless of how skillful they were at football, they still needed someone tall enough to head long balls away.

Wrecka was captain of Hall Park Magpies – and a great centre-back, who won almost everything in the air.

Emma replied: "Yes, I know. Look, it is great but we are still short of players. We still need at least two people, preferably three more.

"Otherwise there's little point turning up."

Charlie looked across the grass where they had played football so often. It was empty. The sun-drenched pitch was beginning to turn a yellow colour as it did almost every year.

The areas they used as regular goalmouths were threadbare – the result of hours spent kicking a ball around.

Those patches would be mud baths by late autumn, he knew.

The heat was going to be an issue.

Charlie had checked the weather forecast earlier and it had predicted that tomorrow would be even hotter than today.

The forecasters suggested it would still be baking hot by the time the game kicked off at 6pm.

They had six players. But they still needed more.

They would need a substitute or two at least – or the high summer temperatures would ensure they ran out of steam in the second half.

Emma looked at the boys.

"Have we tried absolutely everyone? What about Jimmy Welford? Greavesy? Theo?"

Charlie shook his head unhappily. "No to all of them. I've tried all of the Magpies team and a load of the Hall Park Rovers side too.

"They're all away or busy. Even my little brother Harry is unavailable. He's gone away with family friends to a caravan on the coast and won't be back until the weekend.

"He'll be gutted to hear he missed out. There is one bright spot though. Wrecka did say his cousin was staying with them so he might bring him along. I can't remember his name."

Charlie dug into his pocket to find his phone.

"Ha … yes, it is some guy called Mike Battery. Never heard of him and I have no idea if he is any good or not, but it's another body.

"The only person I haven't heard back from is Brian Bishop. I sent him a message but got no response."

Emma held up her hand with two fingers crossed.

"Let's hope Bishop comes through. We need another striker."

Billy walked a few steps around the flower beds and stood in the shade underneath two trees – near one of their usual goalmouths.

Despite the heat, his hair remained immaculate – pasted down firmly on his head.

He turned around: "How are we going to line up?"

Emma had been waiting for that question.

"I've been giving this some thought. It's eight-a-side. Mudder will go in goal – if that bonehead actually remembers to turn up."

The boys sniggered. Mudder could be forgetful at the best of times. Emma continued: "Wrecka and Billy will be in defence.

"We can have three in midfield – me, Charlie and Toby. That leaves space for two strikers.

"If Bishop does come, he can play up front. If not, we'll put Charlie up there and stick this Battery fella into the midfield.

"What do you think?"

She looked at the boys seeking their thoughts.

Billy spoke for both of them. "Sounds like a plan."

5. UNEXPECTED ARRIVALS

Charlie Fry had been playing at Crickledon Rec for as long as he could remember. He loved the park. It felt like home. And now it was under threat. The thought of six weeks with no football at the Rec felt like a lifetime.

Peter and Joe would be appalled. He wished his best friends were here to help get him out of this mess. But they were not.

Emma may have been hot-headed when she struck the deal – but she had a point. It was their home ground and they had to try to protect it. At least they did not have to race to the Rec every night in the hope of getting a game ahead of the Moss Green mob.

One way or another, they would know. They only had six players – possibly seven if Wrecka brought his cousin along. But that was park football. One of the things Charlie loved most about playing at the Rec was you never really knew who you would play with.

Moss Park may have been an unfriendly bunch but they were the exception. Usually small groups of kids turned up with their own ball and ended up in a game with Charlie and his friends.

Others often bowled up purely on the off-chance they might be able to bag a game.

And Charlie thought that may work in their favour today.

He planned to get to the Rec early – before everyone else – and hoped someone who usually would join them could be convinced to give them a hand. As far as plans went, it was a pretty rubbish one. But what other choice did he have?

He had not heard anything back from Bishop. And everyone else was busy. Either they were going to get exceptionally lucky or they would get a pasting.

Charlie arrived at the Rec at 5.15pm. There were still 45 minutes until the game was due to kick off.

Apart from the usual dog walkers and some young kids playing on the climbing equipment at the far end of the park, there was no-one about. The football area was empty. Charlie grinned to himself.

He loved just looking at the grass – a place where so many stories had been made and glories shared.

He dumped his bag and booted the football into the distance. It was time for a short warm-up before the others arrived.

He raced after the ball but stopped midway and began to choke up mouthfuls of thick, green gunge.

Charlie automatically reached into his pocket for a tissue and his inhaler. This wasn't good.

He had done physio earlier and his cystic fibrosis had been behaving recently. But the heat made it tough to breathe.

Charlie could feel the panic begin to rise. He needed to get his breathing under control quickly and forced himself to stay still and remain calm.

Gradually oxygen seeped back into his lungs. Charlie knew it was a bad sign though. He would have to be careful during the match, especially during the first half while the sun was still shining brightly and the temperature had yet to fall.

Frustrated with his lungs for continually failing him, he flicked the magic target in his head onto the tree near his bag.

The target, which was always bouncing harmlessly around Charlie's eyesight, sprang to life immediately. It locked on the tree in a blink of an eye and flashed green.

With a delicate swing of Charlie's boot, the chip flew directly at the tree. It clipped the trunk and dropped down beside the backpack.

"Nice shot, Boy Wonder."

Charlie twisted round to see where the voice came from. He had been completely unaware that he was being watched.

Brian Bishop stood 10 paces behind him.

Charlie could have hugged his friend – even if he had ignored his messages all week. Instead he settled for a high five.

Bishop looked confused: "Now what's all this about a football match? Am I early or too late? I only read your countless messages an hour or so ago."

Charlie laughed. "You are right on time Bishop, believe me."

Bishop looked towards the gates at the top of the park.

"Ah yes. Here comes more of the team, I see."

Charlie followed his friend's gaze.

He expected to see Emma. Or Wrecka. Or perhaps even Mudder.

But it was none of them.

Walking across the grass with a battered pair of ripped jeans and drinking a can of cola was football genius Ad Leeshinski.

The cavalry had truly arrived.

6. FRIENDS AND FOES

"Whassup Boy Wonder? Alright Bishy Boy?"

Leeshinski joined Hall Park Magpies after he impressed at the trials at the end of last season.

Both he and Bishop had been signed up to play as strikers next season – but neither of them had played alongside their new teammates yet.

Bishop looked at the newcomer with a hint of wariness. They barely knew him. This awkwardness did not seem to register in the slightest with Leeshinski, whose swagger was similar to his football style. Charlie could barely contain his happiness – or surprise.

"Ad, what are you doing here? How did you know …?"

Leeshinski stopped Charlie's questions by casually flinging an arm around the Boy Wonder's shoulder.

"I heard on the grapevine that my new mates needed a football genius. I only heard at the last minute so I grabbed my dinner and ate it on the way over."

"Mum won't be too happy about the missing plate, I can tell you."

Open-mouthed, Charlie looked at the stick-thin boy with a shock of dark curly hair on his head.

He never knew if Leeshinski was joking or not.

Bishop shook his head and turned back to Charlie.

"So Fry, who are we playing against?"

Again, Charlie didn't get the chance to answer.

Leeshinski drained the last dregs of his soft drink.

"It's the Moss Green lads. I've seen them play up there and they're pretty decent. There's a big group of them too so I was surprised to hear that we had challenged them. Still, look at our best players. If they score more than two goals, I'll be shocked."

He nodded in the direction of the gate. The rest of their team had arrived and was ambling towards them.

Emma led the way followed by the rest of the gang.

Wrecka was the last one through the park gates – walking alongside a tall wiry boy that Charlie had never seen before.

He guessed the newcomer was Wrecka's cousin, Mark Battery.

Within seconds the team stood together, exchanging high fives and handshakes.

Once the greetings had ended, Emma took control.

"Thank you all for coming.

"We didn't think we would have enough for a full team – so to have enough players for a sub is brilliant.

"We'll take it in turns to be sub to keep our legs fresh. Only Mudder will play the full game."

Nods all round.

Wrecka cracked a lame joke about the forgetful Mudder remembering to turn up and got a playful punch on the arm as a reply.

Emma ignored the fooling around.

"Okay. So Mudder will go in goal as usual. Billy and Wrecka in defence.

"Charlie, Toby and myself in midfield. Where do you play, Mark?"

The tall stranger blushed, clearly nervous with people who he did not know.

He shrugged: "I'll play wherever you need me."

Emma gave a thumbs-up.

"Great. Can you take the first stint as sub? We'll take turns any way."

She turned to Bishop and Leeshinski with a big smile.

"And you two up front then!"

Bishop grinned back.

Leeshinski was not listening.

He lazily juggled the football that Charlie had brought with him and spoke as he showed off his awesome skills.

"It is a good job I came because – by the looks of things – you are going to need some real magic tonight."

Emma pulled a face of confusion. She opened her mouth to ask Leeshinski what he meant … and stopped.

The opposition approached. And there were loads of them – at least 15. They were mainly on bikes and skateboards – shrieking and whooping as they moved through the park.

Emma let out a loud groan of despair as she saw the two people leading the large Moss Green gang up the hill.

Kev Dewis was at the front, as she'd expected.

But it was the sight of the boy with a freshly shaved head that caused her pain. It was Adam Knight.

7. TREE FACTOR

Charlie could barely believe his eyes. What was Adam Knight doing here?

The bully had made his life a misery for years – both at school and on the football pitch.

He stole a quick glance at Emma. She looked grim too.

That was not a surprise: she had been sent off for kneeing Adam in the goolies during a feisty match last season.

Before Charlie could say anything, Emma began to stride out to meet the Moss Green team. The rest of the team followed although no-one could keep up with her.

Charlie awaited the explosion as she went toe-to-toe with Kev and Adam.

"No way is he playing," Emma said to Kev, without even bothering to offer any sort of greeting.

They all looked at Adam. As usual, the thug smirked. He looked delighted at upsetting them.

Kev shook his head. "You don't choose our players.

"Adam often turns up for a game with us at Moss Green so why shouldn't he play?

"You've chosen your best players, I assume. Why shouldn't we?"

Emma did not reply. It was a sensible answer and she seemed lost for words.

Adam's grin got even wider. He did not speak. His smile said it all.

By now, the whole Moss Green squad had reached them.

All of a sudden, Charlie felt very outnumbered.

Red-faced with anger but unable to win the argument over Adam, Emma looked at the sea of unfamiliar faces in front of her.

She blurted: "You've got too many players.

"You can't have this many subs! It'll be chaos."

Kev scrunched up his nose.

"Again, this isn't something for you to decide. You didn't put a limit on the substitutions the other day, did you?

"As a result, we've got our whole squad out. We don't want any tired legs out there, do we?

"This park means a lot to us … and we would hate to risk losing it."

Charlie saw Emma's hands turn into fists.

Her temper was already close to boiling over.

She needed calming down.

He checked his watch and spoke loudly.

"Okay. Fair enough. The game kicks off in 12 minutes.

"There are several piles of dog poop at far end of the field.

"I suggest we use this pitch.

"If you put your bikes and bags over there, they can act as the second goal."

Charlie pointed towards two sturdy tree trunks with a large patch of mud between them, which formed the regular goal they always played in.

Kev nodded so Charlie continued.

"It is the usual park rules.

"No off-sides. No throw-ins but we do have corners and goals kicks.

"Subs can only be made when the ball is out of play.

"And if the ball hits one of the branches of the tree, the shot has 'tree factor' and it doesn't count as a goal.

"If tree factor is called, it immediately goes to a goal-kick. Is that all clear?"

Kev gave a mock salute.

"Fair enough, Boy Wonder. Want to tell us how to put on our boots too?"

Charlie ignored the sarcasm and turned to the rest of his team.

"Come on guys. Let's get ready."

They turned their backs on the Moss Green crew and began to walk back towards their own kit in the usual goalmouth.

Charlie was last.

He walked behind Leeshinski, who was busy telling Emma about the greatest goal he had ever scored.

The chat wasn't loud enough to drown out the whisper in his ear though.

Adam Knight got close enough for Charlie to hear him but no-one else.

"Watch your back. It's payback time, Boy Blunder."

8. THE MAGICIAN

There was a minute until kick-off. Players from both teams had pulled on boots or trainers and were ready to go.

The goals had been formed – with a handful of people behind each end to retrieve the ball after every shot. After all, there are no nets in park football.

Some had attempted a half-hearted warm up. Most hadn't bothered – simply deciding to boot the ball around to lazily warm up their muscles.

Emma had their team in a huddle.

"Ok. This is it. You know what's at stake. This is our park – and we don't want to lose it."

There was a murmur of agreement from the boys.

Emma continued: "They are bigger than us. They are definitely going to try to bully us – particularly if Adam Knight is playing.

"Remember, there's no ref so he is bound to be trying all sorts of dirty tricks. Be on your guard when he's around.

"And lastly, we may be smaller than them but, I promise you, we are better than them. Let's show them how to play real football."

Charlie had never heard Emma give a team talk before.

Her best friend Annie was always the one who tried to rouse and inspire them: the natural leader in the group.

Yet Emma was rather good at it too. Even Wrecka, their usual captain at Magpies, looked impressed. They broke from the huddle and took up their places. Battery, as agreed, was the first sub.

Emma went up for the coin toss with Kev opposite her.

Bishop did the honours and flipped the coin. Kev called tails correctly. He chose to kick away from the trees for the first half.

"Come on lads!"

Emma shouted the encouragement as she bounced back to her position. The entire team looked raring to go – except for Leeshinski.

Unlike everyone else who wore shorts, he was still wearing his ripped jeans and, out of nowhere, he had a fresh can of cola.

He slouched forward to take kick-off with Bishop. Leeshinski looked like he would rather be anywhere other than on a football pitch.

Charlie could not stop watching his teammate. He had never seen anyone like him before. Suddenly he knew what was coming.

Bishop touched the ball in Leeshinski's direction and the Moss Green players immediately dived forward to snatch the ball.

And the striker came to life. A quick drop of the shoulder sent Adam Knight and one of the smaller Moss Green midfielders the wrong way.

The movement allowed Leeshinski to dart through the gap with minimum fuss. Kev slid to try to halt the danger but Leeshinski appeared to have eyes in the back of his head.

His long legs dragged the ball backwards and Kev slid past harmlessly, taking the Moss Green captain out of the game.

Seconds later, a nutmeg on Moss Green's big beefy defender, a lad called Benny Tommison, put Leeshinski clean through on goal.

And he was never going to miss from there.

As the rest of the Moss Green team desperately tried to close him down, Leeshinski looked at the goalkeeper … and winked.

Confused, the goalkeeper did not move.

Leeshinski smiled, he flicked the ball with the outside of his right foot into the bottom corner of the goal.

The keeper watched the ball fly into the goal but did not move a muscle.

Charlie had played against the goalkeeper before.

Tall and strong, Shane Waynn was a good player – but Leeshinski made him look like an idiot.

GOAL!

1-0.

And only 10 seconds had gone. Charlie had not even touched the ball. Not that he cared.

He ran at full-speed with the rest of the team towards Leeshinski, who somehow was still carrying his can of cola.

"Yes, you did it! You are amazing!"

Emma leapt on Ad first, shouting at the top of her voice.

As Charlie ran towards them, he noticed Kev spitting dry grass out of his mouth as he got back to his feet.

The Moss Green captain had a face like thunder.

The team congratulated their brilliant goal-scoring hero – but Charlie knew things were about to get an awful lot tougher.

The real match was about to begin.

9. MAN DOWN

The Moss Green players were bigger and stronger than most of Emma's team.

Apart from Bishop and Wrecka, they could not compete in the air.

Kev had seen this weakness because his team's tactics were simple: either pump the ball long and put Mudder under pressure; or get down the wings and whip the ball in at pace.

With there being no throw-ins in park football, the Moss Green wingers could wait out wide without worry about off-sides or marking.

Once they had the ball wide, the rest of the team made a beeline for Mudder's goal.

Wrecka, as usual, bravely headed away his share of crosses but Billy had struggled badly because he was so much smaller.

Toby, Charlie and Emma had spent most of the match watching the ball sail over their heads as the midfield missed out.

And whenever Moss Green put a long ball forward, there was Adam Knight to pick up the little knock-downs and flicks.

It was not pretty but it was effective.

Five times they had beaten Mudder already and it was only 20 minutes into the match.

Adam Knight had bagged a hat-trick, which he gleefully reminded Charlie about as he clobbered him with a late tackle.

But, despite their roughhouse tactics, they did not lead.

It was mainly due to one reason: Leeshinski.

The striker was unplayable.

Moss Green could not get him off the ball.

They tried to kick him; knee him; drag him to the ground.

Adam Knight had even tried to blatantly elbow him in the ribs.

It did not work.

The striker seemed to be two steps ahead of the opposition at all times.

It was like a magician at work.

If his own teammates didn't know what to expect from him, how could the opposition?

To be fair, the Boy Wonder had not played badly either.

A free-kick (which caused about five minutes of fierce arguing between the two teams) had been smashed low past Waynn's right hand and Charlie had doubled his tally with a close-range tap-in after Bishop had beaten three opposition players.

The score was 8-5 to Emma's team.

Leeshinski had scored five.

Charlie had two. Bishop had grabbed the other one.

They had started well.

Battery had taken Toby's place a couple of minutes ago.

The switch was well-timed.

It allowed Battery – who was easily as tall as Wrecka and Bishop – to fit into the defence and allow Billy to move into the midfield.

But the substitutions were more helpful to Moss Park.

They used three of their seven subs – giving them fresh legs across the park.

Charlie looked at the fresh players, who were full of energy and running, with envy.

The awful gunge gurgling in his lungs remained.

And it was making it hard to breathe properly.

He looked over at Toby, sitting behind one of the goals and felt a pang of jealously.

Usually he hated being a sub but today was different.

He would need a rest soon.

Caught up in his own worries, Charlie did not see the tackle.

"OOOWWWWW!"

The Boy Wonder span around as he heard Leeshinski's cry of pain.

He was lying in a heap on the floor near the Moss Park goal – with Adam Knight looking innocently down at him.

10. DIG IN

No-one moved a muscle. The ball bounced away, forgotten.

"I didn't touch him."

They might have believed Adam if he did not have a huge smirk plastered across his face. Charlie ignored him.

He raced to Leeshinski, who was on the floor with one hand over his face and the other gripped around right leg.

"You alright, Ad?"

Leeshinski did not reply.

Charlie looked at Adam.

"That's a red card and a penalty."

Adam guffawed with laughter.

"There's no red cards in park football, you idiot. I barely touched the big baby. It was a dive. He needs to toughen up a bit if he wants to play football."

The thug pushed Charlie who, for once, pushed him back.

He was sick of Adam Knight pushing him around all the time.

"Whoa, fellas," Kev said as he put himself between the two boys.

"Look, we all know there are no yellow or red cards because there's no ref. It is like off-side – you can't have them without linesmen, can you?"

"Referee's assistants," Billy corrected.

Kev rolled his eyes. "Whatever. You know what I mean. It was a bad tackle so you can have a penalty but Adam will stay on. We'll sub him off for a couple of minutes as a peace offering. Fair?"

"What are you saying, you idiot? I never even touched him." Adam did not look impressed. His hands had curled into fists.

Kev ignored him. "Happy?"

Emma looked at Charlie, who gave the briefest of nods. "Yes."

Charlie looked down at Leeshinski. His hand covered most of his face – but he was looking directly at the Boy Wonder.

The boy winked before pulling his hand over his face.

Charlie nearly laughed aloud. No-one else saw.

For once, someone had been even sneakier than Adam Knight.

"Can you play on?" Wrecka asked, with real concern in his voice.

Leeshinski shook his head.

Billy helped his injured teammate to sit on the sidelines as Toby stood up, happy to make a quick return to the action.

Charlie frowned. Deep down, he knew this wasn't right.

Sure, Adam had fouled Leeshinski.

But play-acting and faking injury was the type of thing that Adam and his gang were known for. Cheating wasn't something they did.

It just did not sit right with him – no matter how much Adam Knight deserved it.

Without saying a word, he knew what to do.

Charlie grabbed the ball and spoke in Kev's direction.

"Okay, it was a bad tackle so it is a penalty but Adam can stay on.

"We don't do red cards, after all."

Silence greeted his words.

Then the gloating began. He knew it would happen.

"Good decision, Boy Blunder."

Adam Knight grinned with glee at his escape and rubbed his hands together.

Emma strode up to the Boy Wonder. "What on earth are you doing?"

The words were whispered but sounded harsh. She did not bother to hide her confusion or anger.

Charlie leaned closer to Emma, so no-one could over hear.

"Ad is fine. He's play acting to try to get him sent off. Knight may be a right idiot but that's cheating. I don't feel comfortable with it – and neither should you."

Emma's eyes flashed towards Leeshinski, who was on the floor where Billy had left him.

She blew out her cheeks.

"He's an idiot. Okay, don't miss the penalty. I've got a feeling things are going to get a lot tougher."

Charlie did not reply.

He ignored the gurgle in his lungs, which seemed to worsen every minute. He picked up the ball and plonked it down on a small weed that was about ten paces from the goal.

Three steps back and he was ready. The Boy Wonder blinked and the magic target in his mind sprang into action.

He locked the target on to the bottom left corner of the goal and waited for it to flash green.

It changed colour in a fraction of a second. He stepped up and smashed it past Waynn, who barely moved a muscle.

9-5!

Charlie and Emma's team were flying.

But instead of celebrating, Charlie walked in the direction of Leeshinski and plonked himself down next to him.

He looked up at the puzzled faces of his team, who had followed him.

"I can't play either, at least not for a while.

"You'll have to play with seven players."

11. THE KNIGHT'S REVENGE

"Why are we both sitting here, Boy Wonder?"

Leeshinski did not look in Charlie's direction as he spoke.

Instead his stare was fixed on Adam Knight, who stooped low to score yet again.

It was now 9-8. They led by a single goal.

Since half-time, Moss Green had been taking full advantage of the extra man.

Charlie coughed again and dug into his pocket for another tissue.

, "You cheated. He deserved it. I know that. Don't you think I have wanted to do that to Adam Knight a hundred times before?"

Leeshinski finally turned to look at him. And then – much to Charlie's surprise – he laughed loudly.

"You're right. He is a toe-rag, but I shouldn't have faked an injury.

"He did try to do me though."

Charlie nodded with a grimace. "Why does that not surprise me? He tries to injure everyone. Ask Emma about it some time. But what is so funny?"

"Ah, you want to know the real reason why I decided to come off?" Leeshinski rubbed his stomach as he spoke.

Charlie nodded.

Leeshinski continued: "To be honest, I wasn't kidding when I said I was midway through dinner when the call arrived. I had to come: you lot needed me. However, I was beginning to think my mum's sprouts may be making another appearance if I didn't get a little rest.

"I thought I could sort out two problems at once."

Charlie shook his head with a grin. He found Leeshinski amusing.

Everyone else would have simply asked to be the next sub – but that thought hadn't even gone through his mind.

Leeshinski looked puzzled: "Wait … why are you here with me?"

Charlie spluttered again and grabbed the tissue once more.

"My lungs are playing up. It is easing off though."

Leeshinski watched the Boy Wonder spit into the tissue.

"What's wrong with you?"

Charlie looked at his friend with raised eyebrows.

He thought everyone knew about his illness but, of course, they had not known Leeshinski for long at all. How would he know?

Charlie spoke quietly: "I have a condition – it's called cystic fibrosis. It means my lungs ..."

"... don't work properly. And that horrible green gunge messes up your tummy too," finished Leeshinski, who was now back watching the game again.

"Err, yes. How do you know that?" asked Charlie, genuinely shocked.

Leeshinski shrugged. He still didn't look in Charlie's direction.

"My cousin has it. She's older – 19 now. Exercise is really important for anyone with the condition, isn't it? And, by the way, I think you're an absolute star, even more than I did before."

Charlie was stunned.

Whenever he told anyone about having CF, they never knew what it was, let alone the all the horrible details.

Yet here was Leeshinski, the football genius, trotting out casual facts about CF off the top of his head as he lounged on the Rec's grass.

In truth, it made a nice change.

"OOWWWW!"

Billy had pole-axed Adam Knight, who was rolling around the ground in a similar fashion to Leeshinski about 15 minutes ago.

"Penalty!"

Kev was not arguing this time. Billy tried to claim he was innocent but not even Emma or Wrecka could defend his reckless slide tackle.

Hands on his head with despair, Billy finally turned away.

He was still chuntering about how he won the ball but no-one listened. It just wasn't true.

Seconds later, Kev coolly converted the penalty despite Mudder's desperate dive.

9-9.

The match to win the right to play at the Rec hung in the balance.

Leeshinski turned to Charlie.

"My mum's sprouts are long gone, I reckon. I think it is time for the big guns to get back on the pitch, don't you?

Charlie grinned. "Too right."

Leeshinski stood up and gave a signal to Emma that they were both ready to continue. They were back in business.

12. END TO END

Momentum is a funny thing in football.

Leeshinski and Charlie jogged back onto the pitch as Emma took a turn on the sidelines.

Yet the return of the two star men did not change the flow of the match.

Even though Charlie's team had an equal number of players again, Moss Green still swarmed all over them.

Perhaps the recent goal rush had inspired them?

Perhaps it was their extra substitutes?

Perhaps they had saved their energy in the first half?

Whatever the secret, Moss Green now began to turn the screw.

"Get up! Get out!" Emma waved her arms to encourage Wrecka and Battery to push up to try to win the ball higher up the pitch.

But they were too tired.

Instead they dropped even further back towards Mudder's goal.

Moss Green responded with gusto – even throwing Benny Tommison forward to join Adam and Kev in attack.

It worked.

Yet another long ball saw both Wrecka and Battery jump up to try to head it clear.

They clashed heads and dropped to the floor, dazed.

Tommison could barely believe his luck.

As the ball bounced out down in front of him, he found himself completely unmarked with only Mudder to beat.

A quick swoosh of his giant boot later, the defender smashed his shot straight at Mudder's head as the keeper raced off his line.

The ball cannoned into Mudder's nose before deflecting between the two tree trunks.

GOAL!

10-9.

The defender hared off towards the trees, sliding on his stomach on the turf in celebration. He obviously did not score too many.

Soon he was joined by the rest of the Moss Green gang.

As Charlie watched, he knew they thought they'd won already.

Mudder was up on his feet but his nose was bleeding badly.

Emma came over with tissues.

"Can you manage to play on, Mudder?"

Mudder looked at his teammate's worried faces: he knew they needed him.

He stood up straight and spoke through gritted teeth: "I'm fine. I'm just seeing stars.

"What happened to you two?"

Wrecka and Battery looked sheepish.

Wrecka held up his hand. "It was my fault. I should have called.

"With these extra attackers, they outnumber us.

"I thought Battery had picked up the other fella, but we both ended up with the same guy."

Emma made a signal to Kev that they needed a minute to sort out Mudder's nose.

In fact, the injury was handy for a quick rethink in tactics.

She looked around the team. They looked shattered.

Charlie still looked pale.

Mudder was busy trying to ram a tissue up both nostrils to stop the flow of blood.

Wrecka and Battery continued to rub their heads where they had clashed.

Toby and Billy looked like they'd run marathons.

Bishop slowly hobbled over to them, his legs sore from the constant kicking he was taking from the Moss Green defence.

Only Leeshinski looked fine.

Emma took a deep breath and began to speak.

She said: "Look, forget about that one.

"You're right, Wrecka, there are too many attackers for you to deal with."

Emma adjusted her blonde ponytail. It had turned dark with sweat.

Even the captain was feeling the heat.

She stopped and glugged down a mouthful of lukewarm water.

"Bishop, you drop back into the defence. Play as our sweeper.

"Win those vital knock downs and the second balls that they are picking up at the moment."

Charlie's eyes flicked towards Bishop, who only ever played as a striker.

He simply nodded though, understanding Emma's reasoning.

"Billy, you are the sub until you calm down.

"You've spent most of this match trying to kick people so I think a period to cool off will do you some good."

Billy huffed and stomped over to the side.

He did not look happy.

Charlie did not have much sympathy though.

Everyone had to take a turn – and it was only Billy, Bishop and Wrecka to go.

Emma's eyes followed Billy for a second before turning back to the rest of the team.

After the wild celebrations, the Moss Green players were beginning to take up their positions again.

Mudder's nose was now bunged up with a tissue.

They only had a couple of moments until kick off and there were only eight minutes left until the final whistle.

Emma spoke quickly.

"Charlie, you're up front on your own. Do what you can. We'll get the ball to you and you do the magic. OK?"

Charlie smiled.

Emma knew he was feeling under the weather and was trying to take it easy on him.

She turned to Toby and Leeshinski.

"Right, we are the legs of the team. It does not matter how tired you get. We close them down, we tackle, we block. We chase down the ball together.

"Win the midfield and we win the game.

"And when we get the ball, we get forward to support Charlie. Any complaints?"

Neither of the boys said a word. Both nodded in agreement.

Emma shifted the captain's armband up her sleeve.

"I don't care if you're tired. I don't care if your legs hurt.

"Give everything you have – and more if possible.

"And when you feel like giving up, remember: this is our home that we're playing for today."

13. THE TIDE TURNS

Charlie and his friends had grown up copying their favourite footballers on Crickledon Rec for years.

Now they had eight minutes to save their home pitch.

They were a goal down against a team with fresher legs and booming confidence.

But Emma's words stirred something deep inside them.

Tissues still rammed up his nostrils, Mudder began to come out and claim any long balls arrowed towards his goal.

The midfield chased the ball in packs, hounding the Moss Green players and denying them time on the ball.

This pressure meant the service to the Moss Green frontmen became ragged.

It allowed Wrecka and Battery to go man-to-man and Bishop was free to sweep up any loose balls.

The tactical change worked perfectly.

And, as a result, the momentum of the game began to slowly swing again.

Toby fizzed a shot into the Moss Green goal, which had sparked a mass argument over whether it bounced inside the bike acting as a post or over it.

Park football always has these flaws, particularly when there were no goals or nets.

But the Moss Green team would not accept it was a goal, no matter how much Toby and Emma protested.

Instead they had to settle for the corner.

Charlie stood back from the crowded goalmouth.

He had barely run at all.

In fact, he had been a passenger for most of the second half.

Not for the first time, he wished he could run like the others.

A quick look at Billy on the side-lines sent a pang of guilt through him.

Deep down, he knew he shouldn't be on the pitch.

He watched as the two teams jostled with each other in the penalty area.

There were four minutes left.

Moss Green still led 10-9.

Charlie stood alone.

Only Mudder was behind him.

If Moss Green counter attacked straight from the corner, he could not stop them.

Perhaps he would slide to try to win the ball, but he doubted his exhausted legs would allow him to get back up again.

Leeshinski stood over the ball.

He glanced in the Boy Wonder's direction for a moment and then put both hands in the air as a signal to the players in the box.

Immediately Charlie knew what he was going to do.

He had seen it before … on an ancient game of football in the early days of the Premier League.

Charlie could barely believe Leeshinski was going to risk it but, as soon as the ball was clipped in his direction, he knew his gut instinct had been right.

Taken by surprise, the other players stood and watched as the corner kick went back into the middle part of the pitch.

Charlie was at least 20 metres away from the goal and was nowhere near anyone else.

A flick of his eyes placed the target into the corner of the Moss Green goal. He made sure he kept it low so there could be no argument over height.

With so many bodies in the way, he doubted his shot would reach the goal but perhaps one of his team could scramble home a deflection or rebound.

The target flashed green.

He turned his full concentration onto the ball.

Leeshinski's corner had been clever.

He had chipped high to give Charlie time to get into position but it did not have much pace either so it made Charlie's task a touch easier.

Watching the ball, the Boy Wonder moved towards the front post, moving away from the centre of the pitch.

Moss Green players began to move out to try to close down the danger.

But it was too late.

Charlie knew he had one chance.

He was running towards the ball, so had to hit the volley at the same time as he turned.

It was a tricky move but he had practiced it enough times.

Slowly the ball dropped out of the sky – and Charlie was there to meet it.

His right foot connected sweetly with the ball. At the same time, his hips swivelled and the ball flew off towards the far corner of the goal.

It kept low as it disappeared through the dense crowd of pulled-down football socks and knobbly knees.

Some jumped out of the way. Others watched the spectacular shot with a sense of awe.

Adam Knight stood on the inside of the post.

His eyes lit up as the ball arrowed towards him.

He stretched out his left leg to block the ball.

But the keeper, who stood a metre in front of him, began to move too.

"No. Leave it!"

Adam cried out but it was already too late.

Waynn threw himself in the direction of the thunderbolt shot but could not stop it.

However he did take a touch, which altered the path of the ball … away from Adam's lunge.

The bully ended up in a helpless heap as the ball whizzed past him.

GOAL!

10-10.

The next goal would decide the match – and the fate of Crickledon Rec for the summer.

14. SPLIT DECISIONS

"Charlie … we need you."

Emma pleaded with her friend. But Charlie knew his game was over.

The score was still 10-10. There were only two minutes to go.

Billy was straining at the leash to get back into the action.

And the Boy Wonder could not run another step.

Wrecka chimed in: "Yeah she's right, Fry. It is just one last effort. We've all got to dig in, haven't we? Neither me or Bishop have been subs yet. It is only fair that we take our turn."

Charlie watched as the whole team nodded along as Wrecka spoke. They needed him. But today they would have to do it without him.

Charlie stood up to his full height. "No. I am not kidding around. My lungs are finished today. I cannot run another step. You can do this without me. Now go and win back our pitch."

The Boy Wonder plonked his exhausted body down on the worn grass behind the goal without another word.

Everyone kept looking at him. Whistles came from the other end of the pitch. The Moss Green players were ready for kick-off.

Emma clapped her hands. "Charlie is right. We can do this. We keep the same formation. Billy, you drop into the midfield and Leeshinski, you go up front."

Wrecka clapped too. "Come on lads."

Suddenly they were all clapping. Out of nowhere, belief surged through the team.

"We can do it.

"This is our home ground."

"Let's get after them."

Charlie watched his team-mates race back to their positions.

It felt strange not being in the thick of the action – but deep down he knew he had made the right decision.

Frustrated at conceding Charlie's wonder goal, Moss Green came out of the blocks quickly – trying to grab the goal that would win the game.

Billy, Emma and Toby worked together to close them down but the ball was being launched regularly towards Mudder's goal.

Time and again, the ball was headed away.

But now the Moss Green midfielders ensured they kept possession of the ball.

Up front, Leeshinski was not being given a sniff of a chance.

With only 30 seconds to go, it looked like a draw was the only possible outcome.

Then, with a whoop, Adam Knight nut-mugged Toby.

Then he repeated the trick on Emma.

Billy lost his temper. There was no way Adam Knight would do the same to him. His foot sliced across both of Adam's shins, sending the Moss Green player sprawling to the turf.

"Free kick!"

Every one of the Moss Green players appealed. Even Emma did not complain. Billy did not look at any one else.

He kept his head down and took up his position by the near post.

The free-kick was on Moss Green's left wing. Kev snatched the ball and put it on the spot where the fouled had happened.

Adam Knight stood nearby. He was still scowling in Billy's direction but did not bother to go into the packed penalty area.

It was only those two and the Moss Green keeper that weren't in the area.

Kev wasted no time. With his right foot, he whipped in a wicked cross towards the near post that Billy was covering.

The cross beat the first couple of headers but not Wrecka.

He flung himself full length at the ball and diverted it out of the penalty area, back towards the Moss Green goal.

And Adam Knight was there waiting.

Five seconds to go. Adam smashed it. His anger went into the shot. It went like a rocket. It flew past the crowd of players, rising all the time.

As soon as he hit it, Charlie knew it was a goal. They had gambled … and lost. The Rec was their home no longer. The ball flew straight towards the top corner.

Mudder sprung to his right in a desperate bid to get to the ball. His whole body left the floor as he tried to keep it out. And somehow his right wrist reached the ball.

But the shot was too powerful. He could not keep it out.

15. THE RIGHT CALL

"GOAL!"

Toby threw his hands in the air and did a Samba dance in celebration.

The score was 31-26 to his team: Emma, Mudder and Toby.

Charlie, Wrecka and Billy were trailing badly.

The game was up – it was nearly time to go home.

It was the first time they had played at Crickledon Rec since their big match against Moss Green.

A loud cheer came from the other end of the field.

Charlie twisted round – half of the Moss Green team were celebrating too.

He saw Kev in the distance, who raised a hand in his direction.

The Boy Wonder waved back, happy with the way things had turned out.

It had been close.

They had so nearly lost their pitch on the Rec.

Nearly, but not quite.

Adam Knight's screamer should have won it for Moss Green.

But Mudder's touch had been enough.

Just.

Charlie closed his eyes as he remembered the scene.

"YEESSSSS!"

Every Moss Green player had excitedly thrown their hands up in the air.

Understandably, they thought they had won a great away victory against a team led by the Football Boy Wonder.

But the celebrations were cut short.

It had been Billy who shouted first.

"TREE FACTOR!"

Everyone knew the rules of park football: if the ball touched one of the branches of the tree, then it was never a goal, regardless of how high the ball was.

The tree trunks acted as posts. The ball could hit them and bounce straight back into play with no-one batting an eyelid.

But any contact with a branch or leaf resulted in a goal kick.

It was that simple.

Like everyone else on the field, Charlie's eyes shot to the branch above Billy's head.

And almost directly above him, a branch wobbled where the ball had clipped it.

It was tight.

Adam's shot would have been a goal in normal football.

But this was park football.

It had its own rules.

No goal.

Time was up.

The game had finished 10-10.

And then the arguing began.

Moss Green thought the goal should have stood.

Backed up by the rest of their team, Emma and Wrecka pointed toward the still-wobbling branch that proved it could not be a goal.

No-one would listen to each other.

Finally the bickering stopped.

Kev looked drained.

He turned to Emma: "So what do we do now? Penalties?"

But Charlie interrupted before she could reply.

"It is a draw. So … why don't we share the Rec?"

"You play at the bottom end and we play at the top.

"There's plenty of space – as long as we both play in the direction of the trees rather than sideways."

Everyone looked at Kev.

"No way, Kev. Let's do penalties and send this mob packing," Adam Knight sneered.

Billy snapped: "Shut up, unless you want another slide tackle coming in your direction."

Adam began to move towards Billy but Kev stopped him.

"Fair enough. You had fewer players than us and we still couldn't beat you.

"You've played well enough to keep your turf."

He ignored Adam's complaints and thrust out a hand to a delighted Emma, who had shaken it without hesitation.

The grudge match for Crickledon Rec had ended in a score draw.

There were no losers that day – just an agreement to give each other some space.

The Boy Wonder was chuffed – he had been dreading having to

explain to Peter and Joe that he had lost their football pitch while they were away.

"Charlie! What are you doing?"

Charlie had been in a complete daydream, remembering Thursday's game. He had completely forgotten that he was in the middle of another match.

So when Billy lobbed the ball in Charlie's direction, the Boy Wonder did not move a muscle – causing his friend to shout out in frustration.

Charlie threw a hand up in the air as a lazy apology.

He turned and began to scamper after the ball, closely chased by Emma.

He was home.

Charlie Fry and the Super Sub

1. HISTORY

The two men stood staring at the bright yellow poster on the wall of the Manor Park changing rooms.

Barney Payne, manager of Hall Park Magpies Under-13s, rubbed his chin as he proudly observed the artwork.

He turned to the man standing next to him: "I am not sure you can beat them. The Football Boy Wonder is something else – our club is lucky to have such a wonderful player. He is a rare talent."

Johnny Cooper nodded in agreement and casually ran a hand through his long, blonde hair.

Throughout an impressive professional career, he had played against some of the best players in the country.

Coops, as he was known to fans, had been a decent football player – playing in the Football League for the past decade.

But Charlie Fry, a close friend of his daughter Annie, was like no other footballer he had ever seen.

"True, but he is only one player – and Charlie is not even a teenager yet. We can beat them."

His eyes flashed back to Barney's colourful poster advertising the upcoming club fun day. The big event would feature bouncy castles, a hog roast, numerous stalls, and games.

All the money raised would go towards helping to pay for the club's running costs next season.

But the main attraction would undoubtedly be the club's final game of the season: Hall Park Magpies Under-13s versus the Mums and Dads.

The friendly 'Parents v Kids' match had been a club tradition for decades.

Yet the match was a first for the club's Magpies side because the team had only been created last season.

The match always took place between the end of the season and the start of pre-season training. It was a serious business too.

No kids' team in the history of Hall Park had ever beaten a grown-up team.

Ten years ago, an under-16s team pinched a remarkable draw with the last kick of the match but that was the only time the grown-up side had been denied a win.

Ever.

Hall Park Rovers – the club's original team for the under-13s – had staged its match earlier in the month, which led to an 8–3 win for the grown-ups.

However, Hall Park Magpies Under 13s' team was different.

They had Charlie Fry. And there was huge anticipation among people that the Boy Wonder could make history.

Barney chuckled.

"Records are there to be broken, Coops. You know that. Nobody has been able to stop Charlie Fry so far. Why should our gang of unfit wannabe footballers be any different?"

Coops slapped his friend on the shoulder.

"I know. I can't lie. I'm really looking forward to it. It is one thing watching this kid on the touchline but I want to see how good he is when I'm on the pitch too. Besides, their whole team is decent.

"Obviously Charlie is the standout player but they're a very handy team overall."

Barney frowned.

"I agree. This Magpies team are special. They have quality in every position. Look at the goalkeeper. Darren Bunnell has to be the most unexpected find of the season. I never thought he would be able to cut it but he's proved me wrong. They will take some stopping."

Barney gave a small smile of pride.

He could praise every Magpies player – they had been so impressive in the second half of the season.

They had gone from being rock bottom in mid-winter to clinching promotion by claiming the runners-up spot, only narrowly pipped to the league's top spot by neighbours Rovers.

And Magpies had already strengthened during the summer.

The likes of Ad Leeshinski and Brian Bishop would add more depth to a squad already bursting with talent.

Coops snapped his fingers and broke into a huge grin.

"You're right, of course. It's time we found out exactly how good this bunch of kids is. And I'm thinking about one little player in particular."

Barney sighed.

"Charlie Fry, by any chance?"

Coops grinned.

"The one and only.

"We both know how talented this boy is already – and how much potential he has too. Now we need to prove it."

The idea came to Coops in a rush.

With a loud snap of his fingers, he said: "I've had a rather brilliant idea.

"I am going to take down that poster, old friend.

"We need to draw up a new one."

2. HOLIDAYS

The pen scratched over the paper, slicing through yet another name on the long list.

"How many do we have?"

Scratching his short blonde hair, Charlie Fry did not answer straight away.

Deep in thought, the Football Boy Wonder gazed at the names in front of him before looking up at his friend.

"Annie, we are going to struggle. It is always the same problem in the school holidays – everyone is busy doing something else."

A couple of weeks ago, Charlie and his friends had managed to cobble together a team to face the Moss Green gang on the Rec.

It had been a close thing because so many people were not around during the long summer break.

He clicked his tongue, deep in thought.

"We don't have enough for a team. Everyone is still on holiday or doing something else."

Charlie dropped the pen in frustration. For the past two hours he had been trying to put together a Hall Park Magpies Under-13s team that could play a match in a week. It was no usual match either.

The football season may have been over and pre-season had not yet begun.

But among the glorious summer weather, late sunsets and endless barbecues, there was one last game that still needed to be won.

Charlie had got the better of the demon football manager Chell Di Santos – and, against all the odds, had won the Crickledon summer five-a-side competition.

But this was something else: Hall Park Magpies Under-13s versus the Mums and Dads.

Magpies had not even existed until last season, meaning it would be the first time this match had ever been played.

And the parents were bound to take it seriously.

But the problem was simple: the game would take place in Manor Park next Friday afternoon.

It was only a week away. Could they get enough players to compete?

Magpies captain Wrecka would definitely be missing.

The inspirational skipper was on holiday so Barney had asked Charlie to pull together the kids' team instead.

Barney would manage the grown-up team and the kids would have to look after themselves.

It was a rule that could not be broken: no adults could help the kids' team, apart from the physio.

Yet, despite his best efforts, Charlie still had not got enough players to put out a team.

Thankfully his buddy Joe Foster, the goalkeeper who had been signed by United over the summer, had agreed to manage the team.

But the rest of the sheet looked pretty empty at the moment.

Annie Cooper plonked herself down on the park bench and took a slurp of lemonade.

"You found enough players to see off Moss Green earlier this summer, didn't you?"

As usual, Annie was thinking along on the same lines as her pal.

He had been part of the park team that had ensured they kept their prized pitch at Crickledon Rec a few weeks ago.

Charlie shook his head in response.

"Yes and no, that was different.

"We struggled then too.

"And we ended up using loads of really good players who weren't part of Magpies team last season – Leeshinski and Wrecka's cousin, Mark.

"Even though they have signed up to play for us next season, they cannot play in this one.

"I'm sure the Under-13s versus the Mums and Dads has always been about the current season's players.

"Brian Bishop can play because he turned out for Rovers last year but that still does not leave us too many to choose from."

Annie patted her friend's arm.

"We'll find enough. You know we will.

"Everyone is itching for pre-season training to begin again. The summer is so boring without football!"

Annie got to her feet.

"Look, let's head down to Manor Park and see if anyone is down there. Perhaps one or two of our team will be kicking about?

"I know we've messaged and barely had any responses but, if we see some of the team face to face, then maybe they can help us out too?"

Charlie pulled a face.

"I don't know. It's a right trek over to Manor – it is across the other side of town and it's boiling hot. I can't be bothered."

Charlie found the hot weather hard work.

He could usually hide his cystic fibrosis when he wanted to, but the boiling temperatures made that difficult.

The heat made him thirsty – and that made clearing his lungs of awful gunge trickier than ever.

Also, he longed for the heat to drop a little so he could get some proper sleep.

Annie, as usual, would not take no for an answer though.

"Wrong choice, Fry!"

She grabbed the Boy Wonder by the collar of his sweaty polo-neck T-shirt and yanked him to his feet.

"Oi," said Charlie. "What are you doing, Cooper?"

Annie let him go and began moving towards the gate in the direction of Manor Park.

She spoke as she walked away.

"My dad will want to beat us more than any other parent. I can't let that happen. If you can't sort out a team, then I will. And Manor Park is the obvious place to start."

With a quick wave of her hand, she passed through the gate and disappeared out of sight.

Despite being abandoned by his friend, Charlie smirked to himself.

Annie Cooper never put up with any nonsense.

It was one of the reasons they got on so well.

The Boy Wonder sighed and enjoyed the last few seconds of being in the cool shade.

He didn't fancy hiking across town in this heat.

But what choice did he have?

He grabbed the ragged team sheet and the pen from the picnic table, gulped down a final gulp of warm orange squash and ran to the gate, calling Annie's name as he went.

3. THE BIG PRIZE

Annie and Charlie did not say a word.

They simply stared. The friends stood in the same spot as Barney and Annie's dad had done days earlier.

A poster pinned to the Manor Park clubhouse noticeboard revealed the size of the challenge in the next match.

"Your dad...."

Charlie's words trailed off but he kept looking at the sign.

Annie gulped, unable to hide her shock.

"I know.

"He must have arranged it somehow without me knowing a thing about it."

Neither of them could believe the words in front of them.

The poster highlighted activities – stalls, games, and food – that you would expect to find at a football fundraiser.

In the middle of the paper, the details about the big match were displayed clearly for all to see:

Hall Park Magpies Under-13s versus the Mums and Dads team.
Can our talented kids outfox the grown-ups?
Kick off 3pm.

This part of the day came as no surprise to either Annie or Charlie.

But it was the line underneath that stopped them in their tracks.

It read:

Courtesy of Johnny Cooper, the winners of the above match will be given a special prize – a group trip to a Premier League match of their choice next season.

"So, let me get this straight," Charlie spoke slowly, still unable to take his eyes off the poster.

"Your dad is stumping up for a day out to any Premier League match we fancy? If we win, of course."

Annie replied grumpily: "It appears so, doesn't it?

"Nice of him to tell me about it, wasn't it?"

"Yeah ..." Charlie frowned, "but why would he do that?

"Hall Park has had 'dads v lads' matches for years but there was never anything to play for.

"In the past, it was just a friendly kickabout."

Annie snorted.

"Well, it's not going to be much of a friendly this time.

"My dad has changed all that.

"Man, our team is going to be gutted if we miss the chance to see an actual Premier League match together.

"Can you imagine how great that would be?

"United. City. Rovers.

"We would be able to see some of the world's greatest footballers in the flesh."

Charlie was only half listening.

He had seen his beloved Blues play once before – a few years earlier in a third-round midweek cup game.

The Boy Wonder's heart began to beat faster at the thought of stepping inside the historic stadium again.

The hairs on his neck began to rise.

This was his chance. Luckily, he had his magic power.

The target was still lazily floating in his vision, waiting to spring into action as always.

He barely even noticed it anymore.

The target, which somehow allowed Charlie to kick the ball precisely where he was aiming, was now simply part of him since being struck by that random lightning bolt last year.

Charlie still did not understand exactly how it happened – but he was grateful to have a magic power.

It had completely changed his life, after all.

A thought flashed across his mind.

"Wait, your dad has been a professional footballer for years.

"Have you never been to a game?"

Charlie couldn't keep the amazement out of his voice.

Annie rolled her eyes.

"Of course, I have, you wally. But dad didn't ever play in the top division. I've seen a lot of Championship and league football over the years but never the Premier League.

"No doubt he will wangle a bunch of tickets from friends. My dad does seem to know just about everybody involved in the game."

Charlie smiled but he could feel tiredness creeping up on him.

He moved to sit in the shade to escape the sun's glare.

The Boy Wonder pulled out the crumpled team sheet from his back pocket and groaned.

It was still almost empty.

Regardless of the prize, they did not have a team.

But, before he could say anything, Annie snatched the piece of paper out of his hands and ripped it up.

She walked to the nearest bin and dumped the scraps of paper without a second thought.

Charlie watched her, open-mouthed.

Had Annie lost her mind?

She grinned at Charlie's reaction.

"Don't you see? We don't have to worry about putting together a team anymore, Boy Wonder."

Charlie did not see her point.

He pulled a face instead.

Annie laughed.

"Charlie Fry, you may be one of the best football players ever but you are also a dipstick. Once word gets out about that prize, they will be fighting over a place in our team."

4. CHANGING PLANS

As usual, Annie was right.

Within hours of the poster being put up, messages began to arrive on Charlie's phone.

Everyone desperately wanted to play.

Some on holiday were even trying to get their parents to come home early so they could be part of the match.

Peter Bell was one of them.

The little blonde winger was one of Charlie's best mates and had been a crucial part of Magpies' successful season.

He was on a surfing holiday but was trying to convince his dad to drive back early so they could both take part in the match.

Always feisty and determined, Peter's message had been exactly what Charlie and Annie had expected.

It simply said: "I'll be there. Do NOT start without me."

Charlie hoped Peter would make it. Belly, as they called him, would be an awesome addition to the team.

However, some of the team's key players would not make it.

Magpies captain Wrecka was abroad with his family and not due back for another week.

He would miss out, but he still sent a good luck message to the rest of the team, insisting they could win without him. Wrecka was like that – always thinking of others.

There were other absences too.

Annie's best friend Emma Tysoe was livid when she discovered what was happening.

She was due to be part of a family wedding in Scotland – and, despite her loud protests, was not allowed to miss it.

Annie couldn't hide a little grin as she sat in Charlie's bedroom and relayed the story.

"Emma was not a happy bunny.

"She would not shut up about how unfair it was and she was planning to come to see my dad and ask him what on earth he is playing at."

They laughed at the thought of Emma reading the riot act to Johnny Cooper over a football match.

Charlie puffed out his cheeks.

"Well, it'll certainly be quieter without Emma, for sure.

"Still, we have enough for a team."

Annie beamed, enjoying being correct.

She nudged Charlie in the ribs: "I told you, didn't I!

"I knew they wouldn't be able to resist the opportunity to see a live Premier League game.

"How amazing will that be?"

Charlie shrugged.

He knew the game against the parents would be far more difficult than half of the Magpies team assumed.

"I suppose.

"We have to win the game first.

"And, if your dad is playing, it might be a lot tougher than we all think."

Annie did not answer.

She looked out of the window and twisted her long hair lazily around a finger, deep in thought.

Charlie guessed she was probably thinking about the bright lights and razzamatazz of a top football match.

Finally, Annie came out of her dreamy trance.

"So how are we lining up for the big game then Boy Wonder?"

Charlie went to reply but someone else spoke instead.

"Don't answer that one, Fry!

"That's my job."

They twisted towards the open bedroom door, where Joe Foster stood smiling at them.

Joe had signed for United's famous academy team earlier in the summer.

As a result, the talented goalkeeper could no longer play youth football with Hall Park.

In fact, Joe could not even kick the ball about down the park any more in case he picked up an injury.

But he was planning to be part of Magpies' coaching staff for next season when he had spare time.

And he'd agreed to manage the Magpies Under-13s for one game while Barney took charge of the grown-ups.

Annie grinned.

"Hi Joe!"

Charlie nodded: "All right mate?"

In several bounds, Joe crossed the room and dropped into the comfy gaming chair opposite his friends.

"Yep, I'm fine.

"I hear Barney asked you to pull together some sort of team for this Friday's match?

"How are you doing with it?

"We need a strong line-up if we are going to see that Premier League game next season."

Charlie chucked the sheet of paper towards Joe, who plucked it out of the air without a second thought.

The Boy Wonder allowed himself a small smile – and waited for the avalanche of questions that would be heading his way in a moment.

He spoke as Joe began reading.

"We are all done. Now it's your turn, Foster. Just pick your formation and tell everyone what the tactics are. No pressure."

Joe did not answer. His eyes carefully scanned over the scribbled names on the team sheet. He did not rush. Joe never did.

Finally, he took his eyes away from the paper and looked directly at Charlie.

"Err, Mr Football Boy Wonder? Why on earth are you only down on here as a substitute?"

5. HEATING UP

Annie flung a pillow towards Charlie's head, which he batted out of the way just in time.

She looked mad.

"What?! You kept that quiet, Charlie Fry! Have you lost your mind? Why would we leave our best player on the bench against a team of adults that includes a professional footballer?

"We can't win without you. You know that. Do you want to go and see a Premier League match or not?"

Still bewildered, Annie leapt to her feet and stood with hands on hips, waiting for an answer.

Charlie did not respond. Instead, he wiggled along the bed.

Annie was now blocking the breeze from the electric fan. He needed those cool gusts to ease the summer heat.

This heatwave seemed never-ending. He was getting sick of the sticky weather every day.

He had guessed the entire Magpies team would react like this.

It was a game they were desperate to win and, whether he liked it or not, he was the team's standout player.

Yet this is exactly why he was doing it – for them.

"Well?"

Annie tapped her foot, impatiently waiting for Charlie's answer.

Joe spoke instead. "It's the heat, isn't it? You can't play in these conditions, can you?"

Charlie smiled.

Of course, Joe knew. They had grown up together and he had seen how the extreme heat made Charlie feel poorly.

Charlie cleared his throat: "Bingo. I haven't been feeling right since this heatwave started – and it is slowly getting worse."

Annie put a hand over her mouth in shock, her anger forgotten already.

She stuttered: "Oh, Charlie, I'm so sorry. I … why didn't you … I … didn't realise…."

Charlie couldn't resist winding his friend up a little.

And this was the perfect opportunity.

"And you dragged me over to Manor Park the other day in the burning sun, didn't you? That made me feel so bad…."

Annie gasped and tears began to form in the corners of her eyes.

Joe laughed. It was a deep, hearty sound that broke the tension.

He sniggered: "Charlie, you are such a wind-up merchant.

"Annie, he does struggle in the heat – that is completely true.

"However, I have never known anyone to convince this joker to do anything he did not want to do.

"Don't let him kid you for a moment longer."

Charlie started chuckling too.

"Gotcha, Coops!"

Realising she'd fallen for his nonsense, Annie grabbed the other pillow on the bed and began whacking Charlie with it.

"You are such a toe-rag, Fry! I felt so guilty."

Charlie laughed as he wrestled the pillow away from her.

"OK, OK! I'm sorry – I was just kidding around."

He pushed Annie away and sat on the pillow to stop her from attacking him again.

He cleared his throat and spoke softly: "Joe is totally right.

"It is too hot for me to even think about playing football at the moment. All sport is out at the moment, in fact, unless it's swimming. I sweat buckets even if I am sitting down inside watching television. I struggle to run 10 metres in this kind of heat.

"If I did choose to start, it would be like Magpies having only 10 players for the whole game. And it would make me feel really ill as well."

He glanced towards Joe, who was nodding slowly to himself.

He understood.

Charlie continued: "You have a full team there. They're all good players. I will happily be a sub but the best I can offer is – perhaps – a run out in the last few minutes, when the temps may have dropped a little."

Joe clapped his hands together and let out another booming laugh.

"Thanks for that lovely speech, Mr Fry.

"Of course, I'm not sure you would have made the starting 11 so it is probably for the best that you have volunteered for a place on the bench anyway."

All three laughed. Whether the Boy Wonder played or not, they would be ready for Friday.

6. FANTASY FOOTBALL

Johnny Cooper gazed at the Manor Park pitch with a small smile stuck on his face.

The corner flags fluttered gently in the warm air.

The grass had turned yellow during the hot summer.

Hordes of people were busy setting up the fun day barbecue and activities on the far side of the ground.

But Coops didn't pay them any attention. He had other things on his mind. Coops loved football.

He had played in some of the best stadiums in England but the sight of an empty football pitch still sent tingles down his spine.

The former darling of Hall Park fans, Coops was nearing the end of his playing career.

Last season had been a disaster. A knee injury had stopped him playing before Christmas – and he had been unable to get back in the first team for the rest of the season.

Younger, quicker and hungrier teammates now blocked his path back into the first team.

Time was running out, he knew. Coops' legs no longer moved him around the pitch like they used to.

Now in his mid-thirties, his mind could still play the game as well as ever but his body struggled to keep up.

Perhaps he could drop down the leagues – maybe make an emotional return to Hall Park to play out the final few years of his career. But it was coming to an end soon enough.

Coops sighed. He was going to miss it so badly. Football had always been his life. It was in his blood.

But when the day arrived for him to hang up his boots, Coops knew what he would do. He wanted to become a football manager.

And when he saw young players coming through the system like Charlie Fry, he knew he could guide them.

Fry was a better player than Coops could ever dream to be, but the Boy Wonder still needed help.

Some sensible advice here and there may help Charlie fulfil his undoubted soccer talents.

And today was one of the times that Coops could help him – even though the Boy Wonder did not even know it.

"Penny for your thoughts."

Barney's voice broke through Coops' daydream.

He turned to face his old friend, who lingered in the shade of the clubhouse.

"Is our team ready?" Coops asked the question with a grin.

The teams of grown-ups in these games were always made up of a mixture of wannabe failed footballers and parents determined to embarrass their kids as much as they could.

Barney chuckled. "They are about as ready as they'll ever be.

"Everyone should be here within the next 30 minutes.

"I'll pin both team sheets on the board."

Barney waved several pieces of paper under Coops' nose.

"Have you arranged the other thing that we talked about?"

Coops nodded to confirm the plan was going ahead as agreed.

That was enough for Barney, who turned and walked towards the noticeboard.

Pushing a strand of long hair out of his eyes, Coops took a look at the empty pitch in front of him.

He loved the build-up to a game – even when it was only a friendly kickabout like today. There was nothing else like it.

Now he was older, Coops made sure he appreciated every second as much as possible.

With a final glimpse at the pitch, he turned and trotted towards Barney at the noticeboard.

Coops skimmed over the names on the two sheets before him.

He knew most of the mums and dads playing, as well as the extra friend he had invited to take part in the game too.

The adults' team always struggled for numbers for a full team – but had never been allowed to invite anyone else under Hall Park rules.

However, this was a new event – it was the first one for Hall Park Magpies. With this in mind, he and Barney had decided to bend the rules a little and invite an extra player.

He wondered if anyone would even notice. Probably not.

Happy with his own team's line-up, his eyes began to scan the second team sheet – the kids' team.

Coops' mouth fell open with shock. He turned to Barney, who shrugged. "You have got to be kidding."

7. THE SHOCK

Families crowded around the noticeboard, trying to get a glimpse of the names pinned to the board.

The family fun day was in full swing.

Hundreds of people had turned out for the fundraiser – enjoying the bouncy castles, face painting, stalls, competitions and the huge selection of barbecue food on offer.

The teams' warm-ups had been completed and the players were in the changing rooms, getting ready for kick-off.

The match would begin in five minutes.

Fans had bagged the best spots to watch the game ages ago.

Indeed, the areas behind the goals were packed with families enjoying the mid-afternoon sunshine.

But it was the team sheets that were drawing the most attention.

No-one paid the slightest bit of attention to the grown-up line-up – all the interest was focused on the Magpies team.

It read:

Hall Park Magpies Under-13s v the Mums and Dads
Manor Park
Manager: Joe Foster
1.   Darren 'Mudder' Bunnell
2.   Gary Bradshaw
3.   Billy Savage
4.   Annie Cooper (c)
5.   Jimmy Welford
6.   Theo Tennison
7.   Paul Greaves
8.   Brian Bishop
9.   Peter Bell
10.   Paul Flemmell
11.   Toby Grace.
Sub: Charlie Fry.

Questions swept around the confused crowds.

"Is the Boy Wonder injured?"

"What's wrong with him?"

"Why isn't Charlie playing?"

"Is he going off to play for someone else and we haven't been told yet?"

But no-one had any answers.

Cheers interrupted the mutters as the teams began filing out on to the Manor Park turf.

Clive Cludes, one of Hall Park's many life-presidents, walked on to the pitch with an old microphone.

With his perfect silver hair and spectacles, Clive had been part of the Hall Park set up for decades.

He cleared his throat and his voice boomed out over the speakers: "Ladies and gentlemen, welcome to the first ever Hall Park Magpies family fun day."

A huge cheer greeted his words.

Clive waited a moment for the applause to die down.

He continued: "Thank you very much for turning out in such large numbers to support our team.

"Now, it is time for today's match – Hall Park Magpies against the Mums and Dads.

"Please join me in giving both teams a warm welcome."

Joe led the Magpies team out. Peter and Toby walked next to him.

The boys, who barely reached Joe's shoulders, looked suntanned from recent holidays.

Joe whispered as they emerged on to the pitch: "Belly, I guessed you would make it but Toby, how did you manage to get back here in time?"

Toby puffed out his cheeks.

"It took a lot of complaining and pleading but finally my mum took pity on me.

"My grandparents were coming home today anyway while everyone else is staying at the caravan until next week.

"Nan and Gramp said they'd happily bring me home with them – and I jumped at the chance.

"We left absurdly early in the morning to get here but it was worth it."

Belly chipped in: "I couldn't miss this one. I just couldn't. To be fair, my dad was happy to get up early and miss the traffic.

"And he's a big kid as well so I knew he wouldn't want to miss out on having a kickabout."

Joe clapped his hands on the boys' shoulders.

"Well, we would really have been up against it if you two hadn't made it here. So, thank you."

The rest of the team gathered into a small circle around Joe.

Bishop scratched his head and looked around: "Where's our superstar?"

Joe nodded towards the touchline where Charlie was busy settling down in the shade of the clubhouse.

"He's resting to try to keep cool.

"Most of you will know this but, for those of you who don't, Charlie can't play in this kind of heat.

"His lungs struggle in hot weather and running about playing football is not the brightest idea.

"He'll come on towards the end – but only if we really need him."

Joe paused as Johnny Cooper and his team filed on to the pitch to loud applause from the spectators.

Barney broke away from the line and came over to the Magpies team with an outstretched hand, which Joe shook.

"Good luck today, you lot.

"No embarrassing the oldies too much!"

The coach chortled with laughter and did not wait for a reply, heading back to his own team.

It felt strange seeing their usual manager with another side but the rules were clear: no adults could help the kids' team.

Joe turned back to the Magpies team: "Do we really need the Boy Wonder to beat this lot though?

"Come on. We all want to go and watch a Premier League game next season, don't we?"

Nods all round.

Joe continued: "We are Magpies. We are a great team.

"We are going to have far too much energy for this lot – even without the Football Boy Wonder."

8. NEW FACES

Everyone giggled at the thought of their mums and dads trying to beat them at football.

Apart from Annie. She remained quiet and kept a watchful eye on her dad's team at the other end of the pitch.

Joe did not notice. He was too busy telling the team how they would line up.

With Magpies regulars Wrecka and Emma missing, plus Charlie watching on the sidelines, they had to change their usual formation.

Mudder – who was taking great delight in showing off his trendy blow-dry haircut – would play in goal.

Annie would play as the sweeper with Gary and Billy either side of her in the back three. Toby and Jimmy would be the wing backs.

Theo, Greavesy and Flem would occupy the central midfield positions with Peter and Bishop as the two strikers.

The team's tactics were simple, Joe insisted, as the team listened.

"They are really old. I mean, they are ancient. We can outrun this lot with ease. Keep the ball. Tire them out. Make them chase us. Mudder will be happy dealing with any back passes, won't you?"

Mudder gave a thumbs-up and a big grin.

"Yes, boss. No problem at all."

Toby plunged a hand in the air to ask a question.

"They look a lot taller than us though, Joe."

Joe shrugged. "Keep the ball on the ground then. There's no point in booting the ball high up into the air if we can't win any headers.

"And if they try to use the long ball against us, then Mudder can come out and claim it. Easy."

Everything Joe said made sense. They were ready.

The manager added: "Remember how good you are. Let's do it."

With Joe's words ringing in their ears, the team broke away from the huddle and moved into position on the field.

Annie remained rooted to the spot. She was still staring at the grown-ups' team with a strange expression on her face.

Joe looked at the opposition and then at her, puzzled.

"Are you all right, Coops? What's the problem?"

Annie shook her head. "My dad is the problem."

Joe raised his eyebrows with surprise but did not say a word, waiting for Annie to continue.

Finally, she added: "If I am not mistaken, Skippy Southover is playing for them."

Joe's eyes widened a touch.

Jay 'Skippy' Southover played for Coverton County, a non-league team in a town 10 miles away. They were part-timers but decent players. And Skippy was especially good.

He would be better than anyone else – apart from Johnny Cooper.

Joe stammered: "What is he doing here? With your dad and Skippy against us, we'll never get near them. It's like playing a professional team."

Annie grimaced. "My dad obviously intends to win this game – whether he plays by the rules or not."

Joe totted up the number of grown-ups, warming up at the far end of the pitch. They had 12 players – so only one sub, just like Magpies.

In this type of friendly match, players tended to sub on and off throughout the game.

It gave both teams a chance to rest weary legs, which would be needed in the powerful summer heat.

But players like Skippy and Coops could run and run, regardless of the weather.

Joe felt his stomach lurch.

He realised his tactics were useless. Those two would not get tired even if they played for three hours.

The referee and the linesmen made their way to the centre circle, summoning the captains for the coin toss.

Joe twirled around in a panic.

It was too late to call everyone back into a huddle.

Joe marched over to Barney, who was clapping his team from the sideline.

"Is that Skippy Southover? Why have you got him lining up for you? It's not fair, Barney."

Barney chortled: "Of course, it's fair. We didn't have the numbers – and needed an extra pair of legs in this heat.

"So, we picked Skippy to help us out. You could have done the same thing. We wouldn't have minded."

Joe pulled a face. "What? I thought we could only use last season's players? That's the rule, isn't it?"

Barney smiled again. "Yes. That's always been the rule for Hall Park Rovers.

"This is Hall Park Magpies – and we make our own rules. Best of luck, Joe."

He jogged away before Joe could protest.

Joe blew out his cheeks in anger.

There was nothing he could do about it now.

They would just have to cope until half-time.

Annie began to move towards the centre circle to face off against her dad.

Joe patted her on the back and tried to remain upbeat.

"We can still do this."

He could tell from Annie's expression that she did not agree.

Joe turned away and headed back towards the touchline, unwilling to show his own mounting doubts either.

9. COMEDY KICKABOUT

Charlie knew Joe was angry without his friend saying a word.

Something in the way that he walked told Charlie his friend was seething with anger.

"What's wrong?"

Charlie passed a water bottle to Joe, who joined him under a big umbrella on the side of the pitch.

Joe took a slurp of the water and nodded a thank you.

"He's only gone and pulled a fast one.

"Coops has brought in one of his football mates to win the game and stop us winning the tickets."

Charlie wrinkled his nose in confusion: "Why would he do that?

"It makes no sense to me.

"I mean, he didn't have to offer the Premier League tickets, did he? So why would he then decide to make it impossible for us to win?

"Something may be going on but I doubt it's about the tickets."

Joe took another sip as he listened to Charlie.

He placed the half-empty bottle on the ground and pointed towards the mums and dads on the pitch.

"Boy Wonder, you know the Magpies players and their families far better than me.

"Who are the adults out there?"

Charlie stood up and squinted towards the far end of the pitch.

"Well, Coops is the captain and that is my dad talking to him now.

"He won't last five minutes in this heat.

"He'll be one of the defenders."

Joe snapped before Charlie could finish: "I know that's Liam Fry, Charlie.

"I've known your dad ever since I can remember.

"I don't mean Liam, Coops or Belly's dad either – I'm talking about the others."

Charlie ignored Joe's tetchy tone and focused on the rest of the grown-ups on the pitch.

"That's Mudder's parents Chrissy and Rick over there, talking to Bradders' dad Sim. It looks like those three are in defence with my dad.

"Oh, they've got Big Jim – the guy with the bushy beard – and Billy's mum Janet in the midfield alongside Coops.

"The goalkeeper is my mum, as you well know, but I'm not too sure about the forwards.

"Theo's dad Ian, or Big E as everyone calls him, is one of them. I'm pretty sure he'll be the centre-forward along with Belly's dad.

"And the woman standing on the half-way line looks similar to Bishop's mum but I can't be sure.

"As for that other guy, I have no idea. I don't think I've seen him before."

Charlie and Joe watched the stranger amble off the pitch, casually kicking the ball into the air with ease.

He was a proper player – even an idiot could work that out.

Charlie scratched his head: "He looks like ..."

"... Skippy Southover?" finished Joe. "Annie says it is anyway."

Charlie could not hide his shock.

"No way! We can't play against him and Coops."

Everyone knew Skippy.

He should have been a professional footballer but he had always been too selfish on the pitch.

He was the striker who never passed.

He never looked to help his teammates. In his mind, Skippy was the world's greatest player and wanted all the glory to himself.

Every manager had warned him. His teammates raged at him for hogging the ball all the time. Fans groaned at his lack of passing.

But Skippy did not listen to any of them.

And he missed his big chance as a result.

Skippy was a good guy. Everyone liked him and he still played football at a decent level.

But Skippy never had the career that his natural skill deserved.

Now about two stone overweight and a blonde haircut that looked like he had been pulled backwards through a hedge, Skippy had finally understood that football was a team game.

But it was too late for him now.

He was the story of the golden boy who got it badly wrong.

And now – for some reason no-one could quite understand – he was lining up against Magpies.

It was going to be a tough one. Applause rang out as the two teams lined up, with the grown-ups kicking off.

Coops knocked the ball back to Big Jim with a swagger.

The beardy midfielder kept the ball for a moment, took a look up before launching it high in the direction of Big E.

The ball went into the air and was quickly lost in the sun.

"Keeper's!"

Mudder followed Joe's instructions to the letter.

He charged out of his goal to punch the ball.

But the sun's glare caught out the Magpies goalkeeper.

Mudder raised his fist to punch the ball clear but could only watch in horror as it sliced off his glove towards the Magpies goal.

It bounced towards the empty net before Annie raced in to hack it off the goal line in the nick of time.

"Wake up, Magpies! We are not giving up those tickets without a fight," she shouted as a red-faced Mudder mumbled a grateful thanks.

Annie barked out instructions for the team to get into their defensive positions for the corner.

It did not matter.

Johnny Cooper pinged a high cross towards the back post where Big E was waiting, completely unmarked.

He rose superbly and nodded the ball past a helpless Mudder.

The header smacked the inside of the post and bounced into the net. Not one Magpies player had moved.

1–0.

Joe blew out his cheeks as his players began blaming each other for failing to pick up the striker.

"This could be a very, very long afternoon with comedy defending like that, Charlie.

"This game – and those Premier League tickets – could well have been lost already."

10. NEVER GIVE UP

Joe was wrong.

After all, Magpies were not an ordinary team.

They did not just roll over anymore, particularly with the likes of Annie, Bishop and Peter in the line-up.

Despite the calamity of the goal, the team came roaring back with a passion that left the adults chasing shadows.

It was Bishop who bagged the much-deserved equaliser.

Peter skipped past Billy's mum with ease before sliding a precise through ball inside the penalty area for his strike partner.

Bishop was aware that Coops was close behind him, planning to slide and block his effort.

But Bishop was too clever.

He took the ball in his stride with a delicate first touch and, as he ran into the penalty area, prepared to shoot.

As expected, Coops slid to make the interception … and Bishop deftly sent him the wrong way with a clever back heel.

He thumped the ball past Charlie's mum Molly with ease as the crowd roared their approval.

1–1.

Bishop winked at Coops as the rest of the Magpies team mobbed him in celebration.

Coops nodded towards the boy but his face was like thunder – he wasn't used to being outwitted by youngsters on a football pitch.

But Magpies were not finished there.

Straight from the kick-off, Theo won the ball from his dithering dad in the centre circle and released Peter on the right wing.

He skipped by Bradders' dad with ease before being sent sprawling by Mudder's mum Chrissy inside the penalty area.

"Penalty," roared every one of the Magpies players and almost all of the crowd.

The ref agreed and pointed to the spot with no hesitation.

Annie made no mistake with the penalty.

The Magpies stand-in skipper calmly sent Charlie's mum the wrong way with the spot kick.

2–1.

And the score stayed that way until the last minute of the half.

The scorching temperatures had left everyone needing a drink and a rest during half time.

But, as Magpies began to run out of steam, the adult team struck back.

Big Jim took the ball from the goalkeeper and ran into the midfield.

He sidestepped a tired-looking tackle from Bishop before pushing further on into the Magpies half.

A classic body swerve sent Greavesy the wrong way and suddenly a pathway to Magpies' goal opened up.

Annie rushed to close Big Jim down but it was too late.

With the outside of his trusty right boot, he powered a swerving shot towards the top corner.

Yet Mudder was ready.

The Magpies number one threw himself at full stretch to reach the ball and touch it over the bar for a corner.

Yelps of amazement could be heard across Manor Park.

It was a stunning save. But the danger had not passed.

And, once again, Magpies could not defend a set piece.

This time, Coops played a short corner to Belly's dad and Magpies failed to react to the danger quickly enough.

The ball was smashed in hard and low towards the front post where Mudder's dad Rick was waiting to turn the ball home – again completely unmarked.

2–2.

The ref blew for half-time as the adults shared a round of handshakes between themselves for the late equaliser.

Joe and Charlie applauded as their team threw themselves to the ground under the small patch of shade.

They had battled back after an appalling start.

The team, led brilliantly by Annie, had gone toe-to-toe with the grown-ups for almost the entire first half. And they were still in the contest.

But Joe and Charlie knew the hard part was still to come.

11. TIRED LEGS

Joe had to raise the spirits of his team because the late equaliser seemed to have knocked the stuffing out of Magpies.

He clapped enthusiastically: "Great work everyone. If we're tired, imagine how the oldies are feeling right now."

No-one answered. They were too hot.

Every member of the team – even Mudder – looked sweaty and exhausted already, and they still had 30 minutes to play.

Despite the heat, it was obvious fitness levels had dropped dramatically since the last game of the season.

Joe continued: "We are better than these.

"We only need to find one goal and this lot are beaten. They are nowhere near as fit as us."

Joe knew this was true.

A quick glance in the direction of the adult team revealed a weary heap of legs and bodies on the grass.

Most of the adult team were still gasping for breath and drinking gallons of water.

They were struggling badly too.

Joe played his trump card.

"If we manage to find that one goal, then we'll be going to the Premier League match of our choice."

Several members of the team smiled.

Others nodded their agreement.

Joe knew his words had got through to them.

"And we still have the Boy Wonder to come on, don't we?"

Charlie pulled a face.

"Perhaps.

"I reckon I can last 10 minutes. That is the absolute max."

No-one complained.

The entire team knew Charlie well enough to accept his limits.

His health came first – and no-one wanted him to be poorly because of a football match.

Joe smiled: "Fair enough, Fry. I'll be guided by you.

"The way this lot played in the first half, we won't be needing you anyway!"

The ref poked his head under the huge umbrella shading the team.

"Two minutes please, ladies and gentlemen."

Joe and Charlie began walking among the team, helping the players back to their feet.

Words of encouragement echoed in the ears of Magpies players as they walked back on to the pitch.

"We can do this."

"Remember they are more tired than us."

"We're only 30 minutes from winning those Premier League tickets."

"We go again. Believe."

Joe watched the team leave the shade and begin to line up, ready for the second half.

He turned to Charlie.

"Can they do it? They look exhausted already."

Charlie shrugged. He did not know the answer and decided to say nothing in response.

The Boy Wonder scowled as he looked at Skippy Southover, the sub still waiting on the touchline.

Coops' team hadn't made any changes either. Why?

Charlie whispered to Joe: "What is Skippy waiting for?

"If we had a player like that, we'd have him in the team, wouldn't we? It makes no sense.

"Why have Barney and Coops got this guy on the bench if they're not even going to play him?"

Joe did not have time to respond.

The game kicked off and, seconds later, the ball was winging its way towards Mudder's goal.

This time the Magpies keeper got it right, rising above everyone to catch the ball cleanly with both hands.

Being an excellent goalkeeper himself, Joe applauded with gusto.

"Nice one, Mudder," he bellowed.

A long kick followed and, in a flash, the ball was coming back towards the Magpies goal.

This time Annie was there to clear with a last-ditch header that stopped Big E from getting a clean run on goal.

Magpies were under siege.

12. SUPER SUB

The clock said there were 11 minutes left and Magpies now trailed 4–2 against the grown-ups.

A toe-punt from Billy's mum Janet and a long-range screamer from Coops had made the difference.

Both teams looked shattered. Joe turned to Charlie, looking downcast. "Do you want to come on, old friend, or should we just let this play out?"

Charlie grinned. "I will be OK.

"Ten minutes or so is my maximum as I said earlier. I'll cope.

"I'll just try not to run too much out there – Belly can cover my shift as well."

They both chuckled, knowing Peter would not be impressed at being volunteered to do the work of two people – particularly as he had already run himself ragged trying to keep Magpies in the game.

Despite the score, Magpies had battled away with great effort but had enjoyed little luck in front of goal.

Now, with only a few minutes to go, the players were showing signs of running out of legs. It was time to shake things up.

Joe signalled to the ref that he wanted to make a change.

He called over to Flem, who had looked tired since the pre-game warm-up, and indicated Charlie was taking his place.

The pair high-fived with a sweaty Flem gratefully flopping into the cool shade while Charlie raced on to the pitch, immediately feeling the searing heat on his body. He knew he needed to be careful.

A ripple of excitement zipped around the crowd as Charlie took up a position as an attacking midfielder.

The Football Boy Wonder had arrived. But the game didn't start immediately because Barney had also signalled to make a substitution.

Charlie looked over at the adult team with interest.

They had not made a single change. Until now.

Again, he asked himself the same questions:

Why? What on earth were they playing at?

Why did they care so much about a friendly kickabout like this?

He watched as Barney indicated he wanted to bring on Skippy to play the final few minutes of the game.

Janet was the player to make way with Skippy bouncing on to the pitch, taking up a space near to Charlie.

The change meant they had Coops in midfield and Skippy alongside him. They were a formidable duo.

Annie started the game again with a throw-in, which she dropped tidily at Billy's feet.

Billy Savage calmly passed the ball to an unmarked Greavesy in the centre circle, who flicked the ball to Charlie without even looking.

It was a move they had rehearsed many times before.

Charlie knew Belly would be moving off the right-wing touchline before he got the ball under control.

One look. Place the target. A reverse pass would cut the defence open and Belly would be clean through.

The crowd murmured as the Boy Wonder took his first touch of the ball.

Charlie looked up to place the magic target.

But, as he twisted around, his vision was blocked.

Skippy had dashed over to close him down. Charlie had nowhere to go – Skippy was on him too fast.

In desperation, he flashed the target into the space beyond his marker and flicked the ball in the direction he knew Peter would be.

But it was no use. He did not have time and the pass was blocked from getting through. It cannoned off Skippy's legs and bounced away harmlessly for a throw-in.

The crowd groaned.

They had seen Peter in oceans of space and knew a through ball would have set up a goal scoring opportunity.

Charlie put up a hand to apologise.

Skippy ruffled his hair as he jogged back to his position.

"Unlucky kidda."

Charlie swatted the hand away, despite the friendly gesture, and did not reply. He didn't need sympathy.

Skippy grinned and continued to stand close by.

A man-to-man marker. Charlie had never had such close attention on a football pitch before.

Then he realised. Coops had brought this guy along for one reason only: to stop him playing his normal game.

And now everyone was watching to see how he would meet the challenge.

13. THINKING OUT LOUD

The crowd roared as Magpies won a corner.

Charlie took the chance to grab Bishop and Peter as Toby walked towards the corner flag.

"It seems like they have decided to man-mark me," said Charlie in hushed tones so no-one would overhear.

Sweat dripping from his face, Bishop nodded.

"Yes, he did seem to pounce on you the moment you got the ball a few seconds ago."

Belly warily eyed up Skippy, who was lingering not too far away from them.

"What do you want to do, Boy Wonder?"

Charlie spoke quickly as Toby prepared to take the corner kick.

"This man-marking idea is a massive mistake and it offers us a real chance to get back in the game."

Charlie paused to make sure both of them were listening to him.

They were so he continued: "Magpies has never been a one-man team, which is why we have been so successful. I'll move him out of position. You guys look for the gaps that he leaves. I'll find you."

Both Bishop and Peter gave the thumbs-up.

It was not much of a plan, but it was the best he could do in such a short time.

Toby's corner was easily headed clear by Charlie's dad Liam.

Annie collected the loose ball near the touchline and played a sharp pass to Charlie, who was inside the centre circle.

Skippy was breathing down his neck before he even received the ball. Charlie did not hesitate. He laid the ball back to Billy without a second thought. He did not want to lose possession when half of the team were out of position, high up the field.

As Billy hoofed the ball forward, Charlie glanced around and noted his marker remained only a couple of metres away – even though the ball was now in the far distance.

Skippy was sharp, organised and disciplined.

And he had been asked to stop the Boy Wonder.

Charlie's mind raced. He had never backed down from a challenge in his life. And he wasn't going to start now.

He called over to Joe, who was pacing the touchline.

"How long have we got left?"

"Seven minutes," replied Joe.

Charlie waved his thanks. He returned his attention to the match, where Bishop and Jimmy were trying to press the grown-up team high up the pitch.

It was no use. Coops and one of the women passed around the boys with ease and broke forward with real menace.

Coops chipped the ball towards Big E, who had peeled off Toby's shoulder and was charging into the empty space.

Mudder had spotted the danger. The Magpies goalkeeper raced out of the penalty area to intercept the through pass.

Aware he couldn't use his hands, Mudder headed it instead – and sent the ball flying in Charlie's direction.

"Belly!"

Reading the situation, Charlie shouted a warning to his friend before Mudder had touched the ball. Peter would know what to do.

The Boy Wonder took the ball neatly on his chest and twisted to face his marker, who was upon him almost immediately.

Out of the corner of his eye, Charlie could see Coops running to try to close him down as well.

It did not matter. None of them were close enough to stop him this time – even Skippy. And Charlie needed only a split second.

With the ball under control at his feet, his eyes flicked up and the magic target inside his mind sprang into life.

A split second later, the red target locked into the correct space beyond the opposition's defence and flashed green.

Charlie stroked the ball with the perfect weight needed.

Even though the Football Boy Wonder was deep inside his own half, the ball sliced through the mass of bodies in the midfield.

The pass evaded Charlie's dad's desperate lunge and went straight into the path of a flying Peter.

The crowd roared as Belly raced through on goal. The goalkeeper began to move out but did not make it far.

As cool as you like, Belly brilliantly chipped the ball high over Molly's head and casually threw an arm into the air before the ball had fallen from the sky and bounced into the goal.

Seconds later, the crowd erupted as the net rippled.

4–3.

Magpies were back in the match.

14. WONDER

It had been weeks since the end of the soccer season and Charlie had not realised how much he'd missed playing football.

It felt great being out on a pitch again, even if the grass was nearly dead and his game out would only last a few minutes.

Since Peter's wonder goal, the tide had turned.

Coops had pulled almost every one of the grown-up team back to defend their 4–3 lead.

Only Peter's dad remained upfield, allowing Magpies to pile forward in search of the last gasp equaliser.

Two minutes remained.

Charlie dropped back towards the centre of the pitch again, closely followed by his man-marker.

"Skippy isn't even looking at the ball," Charlie muttered to himself. "He is only interested in following me."

Since his assist for Peter's goal, the marker had been sticking closer than ever to him.

It was annoying but Charlie knew he had to be patient.

He was sure he would get a chance.

The sweat had begun to drip off his neck but he ignored it.

As long as he kept finding small pockets of space, the Magpies players would find him with the ball.

He did not have to wait long.

Flustered by the green shirts surrounding him in the penalty area, Bradders' dad smashed the ball out of the danger area.

He got a great connection – perhaps a little too good.

The ball flew flat and straight towards Skippy.

And, as Charlie had spotted only moments earlier, his marker was not watching the ball.

Only a scream from Coops alerted Skippy to the incoming ball that was flying towards him like a missile.

If he had been fully concentrating on the game, Skippy would have known that all he had to do was duck.

Then the ball would have shot over him and fallen straight into the path of Peter's dad for a counter attack.

But he had been concentrating on Charlie too much.

And a lack of game awareness cost him.

At the last moment, Skippy twisted to take the ball on his chest but his reactions were a fraction too late.

The ball awkwardly struck his right shoulder and flew into the air.

This was the moment Charlie had been waiting for.

He watched the ball and knew he needed to time it perfectly.

In a flash, Charlie moved forward and, as the ball came down, he nodded the ball forward to ease away from the opposition player.

Skippy, who was now hopelessly off-balance, swung a leg to stop the Boy Wonder but ended up in a heap on the ground.

Charlie's touch took the ball away from his marker and now there was no-one in front of him.

Everyone else was still inside the penalty area.

Coops and Big Jim both spotted the danger and dashed out to try to close down the space with giant strides.

It was too late.

Charlie finally had a sight of goal.

A split second later and the magic target inside his mind locked on to the top corner of the goal.

Then it flashed green.

Charlie's eyes immediately returned to the ball bouncing a metre or so away from him.

With a grunt of effort, the Boy Wonder hammered the ball with the most powerful kick he could manage.

Charlie struck it perfectly.

The ball flew straight over Coops' desperate slide tackle and comfortably above the heads of defenders and attackers.

A roar erupted from the spectators behind the goal as the ball crashed into the top corner of the net.

Charlie's mum had not even moved in goal.

"Charlie, Charlie, Charlie...."

The crowd sang the Boy Wonder's name with gusto.

Their football superstar was back.

Charlie Fry stood in front of the crowd with both arms aloft with the biggest grin on his face.

Moments later he disappeared.

Annie and Peter had dragged him to the floor.

Then the rest of his excited teammates piled on top of the Football Boy Wonder in wild celebration.

15. HANDSHAKES

There was no time for kick-off.

Three blasts from the ref's whistle ended the game before the Magpies players had even managed to untangle themselves from the pile on top of Charlie.

The game was over. It had finished 4–4.

Charlie's dad Liam gave his son a great bear hug as the two sets of players began the end-of-game handshakes.

"Well done, son. That was incredible."

Charlie pushed his sweaty dad away. "Gerroofff dad. Thanks … but you stink. Time for a shower."

Liam laughed heartily: "You are a cheeky devil. Anyway, congratulations again, that was some equaliser."

Beaming with pride, his dad moved in the direction of Mudder.

Coops was next up. "Charlie Fry. Wow. Just wow."

Charlie shrugged and tried to ignore the blushing that he could feel spreading across his face.

"Thanks, Coops."

Coops shook his hand and pulled him closer. "I knew you were good. I never realised quite how good you are. And today may just change everything."

Charlie pulled a face, completely puzzled. Today's game was a friendly. Nothing more. It was nice to have the bragging rights over his mum and dad, of course, but it didn't mean anything more than that. He opened his mouth to ask what Coops meant but the older man had swiftly moved away.

Charlie shrugged. He would have to corner Coops later – probably with Annie's help – and ask him what he meant.

The Boy Wonder spent the next few minutes shaking hands and being congratulated on his last-gasp goal.

Skippy was last to offer his hand with a big grin. "That was very impressive, young man. You've managed to make me look a right mug today."

Charlie giggled in response.

Skippy rolled his eyes and continued: "I suppose I should be used to it.

"You are not the first and you certainly won't be the last either.

"I didn't think a kid could show me up on the football field, but I've been proved wrong today. Well done."

Their chat was brought to an abrupt end with the crackle of the club's old speaker system.

They turned and saw Barney taking the microphone with Coops and Clive standing a couple of paces behind him.

He addressed the crowd: "Ladies and gentlemen, boys and girls.

"Thank you for coming today to the first-ever Hall Park Magpies family fun day. I hope you enjoyed – and I am sure you will have – that thrilling game. A 4–4 draw is quite a result for both sides."

A polite round of applause greeted Barney's words.

"As you know, a very good friend of our club – Mr Johnny Cooper – gave the kids' team the chance to win Premier League tickets to a game of their choice, if they managed to win the game.

"That did not happen – even if our team of youngsters gave the grown-ups quite a fright with that late thunderbolt."

A few jeers came from the crowd, unhappy that Magpies were going to miss out on the big prize – despite an incredible performance.

Barney raised a hand to silence the moaners.

It worked and he continued: "However, I have spoken to Coops and he has agreed with me that the Under-13s deserve something for their efforts."

A ripple of excitement went around the Magpies team. Every single player was looking at Barney, hanging off every word.

Barney smiled kindly. "So, we have decided we will take the Magpies to a Premier League game next season...."

Gasps of excitement came from across the pitch and stands.

Barney continued: "... but we have decided to choose the game instead."

The Magpies manager knew all eyes were on him.

He paused for a second before speaking into the battered microphone once more: "How does United v City sound?"

Barney may have continued talking but no-one heard him.

Cheers and wild applause erupted from the crowds around the pitch.

Water covered the pitch as bottles were chucked in the air in celebration. And for the second time in five minutes, the Magpies team were in a giant pile. They had done it.

16. SCOUTED

The three men stood in the Magpies clubhouse.

They had waited for everyone else to leave before having this conversation.

"Well?"

Coops could not help but smile as he asked the question. He knew the answer that was coming.

"Yes, very impressive."

The man replied while he used a corner of the day's programme to pick out the remains of a greasy burger from his teeth.

He was a small and tubby man, who exercised too little and spent too much time driving around the country eating rubbish food.

"This Fry kid definitely has some skill. There is no doubt about it. His equaliser was a joy to watch.

"However, this was only a friendly match so it doesn't tell us much.

"And he was playing against a load of tired parents, who had been running about in the heat for 50 minutes, while he turned up as fresh as a daisy."

Coops had anticipated these comments days earlier. He had planned for it.

He shot back: "Good point.

"That was one of the reasons that we offered the incentive of Premier League tickets.

"We tried to give the game an extra edge – rather than a pointless end-of-season friendly.

"And, as soon as Charlie came on to the pitch, we made a change too. You may have noticed?"

The man tutted but Coops continued nonetheless.

"Skippy Southover is a semi-professional footballer. And a really good one at that.

"I spoke to him before we came in here and he admitted he couldn't get near Charlie.

"He was playing at 100 per cent and was instructed purely to man-mark Charlie, nothing else.

"Despite this attention from a proper adult footballer, the Boy Wonder made one and scored another."

Coops clapped his hands together.

He knew many people at the Football Association but he had never pulled any strings to get an England scout to a game before.

Until now.

Geoff was one of the FA's scouts for the region.

He was a nice guy and truly loved football – but you had to be special to gain his interest.

He frowned: "This is all rather unusual.

"Charlie does not play for a club's academy or at a high enough level to be on our radar. I assume he's had clubs sniffing around?"

Coops shrugged: "Yes, but he's turned them all down.

"He's waiting for one club, I reckon.

"His beloved Blues, but they're about the only Premier League club not to have come knocking so far."

Geoff nodded his understanding and wrote a couple of notes into a tatty old notebook with a brown cover.

He looked at Barney. "Are you his club manager? Do you agree with Coops on this kid's potential?"

Barney puffed his chest out, pleased to have been asked his opinion.

"Yes, I do. I have been working in the game for 40 years and I have never seen a child with such ability.

"It's not just the wonder goals.

"Incredibly, we see that kind of thing from him all of the time. Today's effort wasn't even among his top 10 goals.

"He has something else.

"He is not the quickest. And he certainly isn't the biggest.

"But he thinks like a top footballer. It's the way he moves.

"Charlie Fry thinks three steps ahead of other people – and then has this incredible ability to deliver the right pass or shot at exactly the precise time.

"You can't teach that."

Geoff studied Barney closely. He could see the passion in the old man's eyes as he spoke.

The scout said: "He has the attributes to play at a high level – perhaps even the very highest in the game.

"But what about his illness? This fibrosio…."

Coops stepped in.

"You mean cystic fibrosis? Yes, Charlie does have a serious

condition and it needs to be managed carefully.

"You cannot overburden him or expect too much from him.

"He has medication to take day and night and his health must always, always come first."

Barney added: "But why should that stop him?

"As long everyone is aware of his condition and helps him manage it, why can't he be allowed to be the best he can be?

"Charlie doesn't let his illness stop him.

"He may require a bit more understanding than other players but his talent and dedication make up for it.

"All he needs is someone to believe in him – as we have."

Geoff did not reply straight away.

He scribbled several extra notes in his notebook before re-reading his words and tucking the pad back into his pocket.

"Fair enough. I agree – Charlie Fry is special.

"Rarely do we see that type of vision in someone so young.

"I'm glad you called me here today, gentlemen.

"We have an Under-16s European Championship coming up later this year.

"I will speak to the manager tonight and we will take a proper look at the Football Boy Wonder there."

Coops and Barney both beamed.

Their plan had worked.

The Boy Wonder would be going to the Euros next month – playing with kids three or four years older than him.

It would be a heck of a challenge.

Coops scratched his head, unable to keep the smile from his face.

"Err, one more thing, Geoff.

"I don't suppose you've got 20 or so spare tickets for United v City next season?"

ALSO BY MARTIN SMITH

The Football Boy Wonder Chronicles is a series of short stories featuring Charlie Fry.

All of Charlie's earlier adventures are listed below:

The Football Boy Wonder

The Demon Football Manager

The Magic Football Book

The Football Spy

The Football Superstar

The entire Charlie Fry Series is available via Amazon in print and on Kindle today.

Martin has also written a Halloween story for older children:

The Pumpkin Code

Follow Martin on:

Facebook
Facebook.com/footballboywonder

Instagram
@charliefrybooks

ACKNOWLEDGMENTS

The Football Boy Wonder Chronicles is a collection of stories that I loved writing. The ideas for them came to me as I wrote the main Charlie Fry Series.
None of them fitted into the series overall storyline – but I wanted to share the Boy Wonder's extra adventures nonetheless.
Numerous people provided a helping hand to make the book. In no particular order, they are:

Man of mystery Mark Newnham juggled secretly getting married while creating the book's brilliant cover.
Football genius Alicia Babaee for her outstanding copy editing and no-nonsense straight talking.
Richard Wayte proofread the final version to straighten out the inevitable grammatical wrong turns.

ABOUT THE AUTHOR

Martin Smith lives in Northamptonshire with his wife Natalie and daughter Emily.
He is a qualified journalist and spent 15 years working in the UK's regional media.
He has cystic fibrosis, diagnosed with the condition as a two-year-old, and wrote the bestselling Charlie Fry Series to raise awareness about the life-limiting condition.
He writes children's books in his spare time, mainly, to keep away from the fridge and the Xbox.

COPYRIGHT

Printed in Great Britain
by Amazon

34388793R00076